The Rise of Lazarus

Books by B. W. Jackson

The Rise of Lazarus Series
Book 1: The Rise of Lazarus

Coming Soon!
Book 2: The Brotherhood of Barnabas
Book 3: The Cave of Cleopas

For more information
visit: www.SpeakingVolumes.us

The Rise of Lazarus

B. W. Jackson

SPEAKING VOLUMES, LLC
NAPLES, FLORIDA
2025

The Rise of Lazarus

Copyright © 2025 by B. W. Jackson

All rights reserved. No part of this book may be reproduced or transmitted in any form or by any means without written permission.

ISBN 979-8-89022-220-6

For my mother and in memory of my father

Chapter One

The Holocaust Survivor

Trudging through the February slush, Aaron regretted setting up a meeting with Professor Freeman. He rarely went out of his way to meet with professors, and never with a professor he hardly respected. Since the first day of class, Aaron had thought of Professor Freeman as a charlatan. His introduction to the course had been fraught with clichés and absurd claims, meant to get the attention of the students. He seemed to have the naïve enthusiasm of a freshman philosophy student, and an equal depth of thought.

Aaron's opinion was confirmed in talking to his classmates, some of whom had had Professor Freeman before. One had taken several courses with him because she was certain he hadn't read a single paper of hers, and yet she still wound up with a good grade at the end of each semester. Professor Freeman was notorious for his lazy grading. Regardless of what students thought of his academic qualities, they all agreed on that point. Some believed he was brilliant, others believed he was a fraud, but everyone knew he did as little work as possible.

Thinking back to the previous lecture, Aaron rued accepting Professor Freeman's open invitation. He regularly offered to meet with students to discuss topics he couldn't afford to spend time covering. Usually they were provocative subjects, undoubtedly involving the kind of conspiracy theories the professor found more fascinating than the actual history. Aaron had foolishly taken the bait and approached Professor Freeman at the end of class.

In Aaron's defense, the subject was of personal interest. Professor Freeman, deviating from his lecture on the Heidegger and Hannah

Arendt affair, had told the class in his usual energetic and farcical manner that he had an incredible story about a Holocaust survivor he had met while working on his doctorate at Princeton. Almost all his stories seemed to mention either his undergraduate days at Dartmouth or his time at Princeton or his post-doc fellowship at Harvard. Even with his personal connection to the Holocaust, Aaron should have been more wary of setting up a meeting, especially given the flippant way in which Professor Freeman had brought up a Holocaust survivor. He could be fairly certain that the professor wouldn't have anything meaningful to share. At best Aaron would likely have to listen to some fanciful tale.

Aaron found Professor Freeman already seated in a corner at the small campus café, a mug of coffee beside his laptop. The professor glanced up and hailed him and turned back to his computer. Aaron silently slid into his chair, still in his parka, as Professor Freeman continued to work on his laptop. Aaron sat motionless, staring at the ground, until he heard the laptop shut.

"Is this your first time taking a course with me?" asked Professor Freeman. "I haven't really noticed you in class. You don't stand out much."

"Yep. First time."

And last time, thought Aaron. He smiled at the professor as he imagined telling his classmates about the encounter.

"Where are you from?" the professor asked.

"Outside Boston."

"Okay. Whereabouts?"

"Brookline."

"Sure, I know that area very well."

Aaron nodded politely.

"I don't know if I've mentioned it in class, but I did a post-doc fellowship in Boston—at Harvard, actually."

"Oh, is that right?" said Aaron.

Professor Freeman went on to give a sauntering summary of his academic career. Aaron alertly nodded along, widening his eyes in exaggerated awe as the professor related anecdotes involving obscure academic figures, perhaps famous in university circles, who had praised him and helped him along the way. Meanwhile, the minutes ticked past.

"And that's how I ended up in these wintery wilds," concluded Professor Freeman.

Aaron glanced up at the clock as the professor motioned to the snow that had begun to fall outside the window.

"Interesting," said Aaron.

"But of course that's not why you're here," said the professor with a flourish. "You're here to find out more about the mystery man."

"Right . . . The Holocaust survivor."

"Yes, the Holocaust survivor. But he's much more than that," Professor Freeman said with a gleam in his eye. "Let me ask you, Aaron. Have you ever read the Gospel of John?"

"No, not all of it."

Aaron fidgeted, looking back at the time. He should have already left for class and still he hadn't learned anything about the Holocaust survivor.

"I must recommend that you do. It is a fascinating book—truly a work of literature—fascinating," he said. "But there is one story in that book that I must tell you about."

"I see."

"Yes, to be exact, there is one figure in that book that I must tell you about."

"I'm very sorry," said Aaron. "I really have to go. I have a class at four."

Professor Freeman watched in bewilderment as Aaron shuffled out from behind the table.

"Oh."

"I'm sorry. I thought I mentioned it. Could we continue another time?"

"It must have slipped my mind. Certainly, we could."

"No, it's my fault. I'm sorry to be rude."

"Listen," Professor Freeman said. "I want you to do something for me. Go to the library and find a copy of the New Testament. Any version will do. Find the book of John and read Chapter 11. Let me know when you've done that, and we'll get another coffee."

"Okay, thanks. I'll be in touch."

"John Chapter 11," Professor Freeman called after him. "That's where the story begins."

Aaron pulled his hood over his head and went out into the snow, clenching his teeth in frustration. Just as expected, Professor Freeman had droned on about nothing in particular, aside from his own achievements, and now he was going to be late for class. Perhaps that sort of performance was charming to some people, but for him it had been completely worthless. The professor had filled nearly half an hour with an egocentric monologue and some nonsense about the New Testament. Aaron decided there was no way he would take the time to look up some random scripture, and he definitely wouldn't be getting another coffee with Professor Freeman. The last thing he needed was another homework assignment. His real homework assignments were enough of a waste of time!

Aaron was far from an enthusiastic student. In his first three years at college, aside from his meeting with Professor Freeman, he had only visited professors when forced. His mother, a professor, assured him that he was a professor's nightmare. On average, Aaron estimated that he had completed about a quarter of the assigned work, and yet he had a perfect GPA. The trick was that he completed every piece of assigned work that counted, and he had a knack for retaining the information that mattered. In truth, he had a knack for retaining any bit of information at all.

In high school, his poor work ethic had been his downfall. He drowned in the piles upon piles of mindless work that counted so much toward his grades. He got into a few colleges based purely on his potential, which was far from insignificant. He had aced or nearly aced every exam he had ever taken. And his college essays and writing samples were brilliant. More than one admissions director had written him a personal note, stating that they had never let in a student with as poor a record in the classroom. But, in short, they simply could not deny him.

Aaron didn't lose his penchant for indolence when he got to college, but he found the system was far more accommodating to his particular academic style, as he called it. His mother, again, assured him that laziness was not an academic style. During his first semester, he took a Renaissance art history course in which the only graded assignments were two papers and a final exam. He could write the papers without doing a page of reading. He merely regurgitated the professor's words, because he could remember every lecture nearly verbatim. The final exam, in addition to essay questions, consisted of a hundred Renaissance artwork identifications, all of which the professor had gone over in class. Aaron didn't even bother to review the images the night before. Sitting the exam, he could summon every detail of the year and the artist, as if flipping through a catalogue in his head. Aaron was arguably the best mind and the worst student in the entire undergraduate college.

That week, Aaron scarcely thought of his meeting with Professor Freeman. He relaxed over the weekend and, putting his assignments off until the last minute as usual, he only got back to the library on Sunday evening. Settling into a carrel, he tried in vain to force himself to work. He opened a book and read a page, closed it and tried another book. Putting that book aside as well, he swung open his laptop and checked his email one more time and looked at the basketball scores. In his unremitting procrastination, he remembered the passage Professor Freeman had told him to read and looked it up online.

With faint curiosity, and some reluctance, Aaron read the chapter from start to finish, wondering why specifically Professor Freeman would have insisted he look it up. It appeared to be a sort of sophisticated fairy tale, which was exactly what he might have expected. He imagined that Professor Freeman, a typical faux intellectual, probably had some asinine theory about an affair between Jesus and Mary Magdalene. He only took a moment to dwell on what he had read, dismissing it as nonsense. Aaron shook his head as he thought of the way Professor Freeman sat in the campus café, the way he smugly sipped his coffee. He put the Bible passage out of mind and was finally able to begin his homework.

Chapter Two

Two Gruesome Tales

On Monday, Aaron had a full day of classes and homework, and yet he grew slightly more curious. His interest was piqued, undeniably. The Bible story kept running through his mind and he wondered increasingly why Professor Freeman had told him to read it. Begrudgingly, Aaron succumbed to his curiosity. At the end of lecture that week, he approached him. Initially the professor acted as though he didn't recognize Aaron, and then a grin crept across his face. Before Aaron could say anything, the professor addressed him.

"You've read it, then?"

"Well, yeah, I just got around to it."

"Good. I'll meet you at the café tomorrow at the same time."

Before Aaron could respond, Professor Freeman had turned to another student. Aaron walked away without answering, again annoyed at himself for setting up a meeting. It happened to be that his schedule was free at that time, but Professor Freeman couldn't have known that.

The next day, Aaron found Professor Freeman in the same place he had found him before, his computer open with a coffee beside him. When he saw Aaron, he closed the computer and pushed it aside.

"Good to see you again, Aaron."

"Thanks again for making the time."

"I knew you wouldn't be able to resist."

"You were right," Aaron conceded dully.

"Before we begin, may I ask why you have such a particular interest in the Holocaust?"

"Well, I am Jewish."

"I had guessed that. As am I. Anything else?"

"And my grandfather is a Holocaust survivor."

"I see," said the professor. "You know, most people know that the Jews have a long history of being victims, but there's another way of looking at it. Yes, of course, they have a long history of being victims, but they also have a long history of being survivors. People usually only think of the survival of the Jews in general, or of Holocaust survivors specifically."

"That's true," said Aaron.

"Every era of persecution creates a generation of survivors," went on Professor Freeman. "Let me give you an example. As you probably know, Christians consistently persecuted Jews in the Middle Ages. In fact, many of the Crusades took place not in the Middle East, but right in Europe, against the Jews. The idea of deicide was widely accepted—that is, the idea that the Jews killed God, because they killed Jesus. Then there were the blood libels—accusations against Jews for killing Christian children and using their blood ceremonially."

Aaron nodded, vaguely familiar with the history. Professor Freeman paused and took a deep breath, adopting the measured tone of a raconteur.

"The case I am going to tell you about took place in a small town along the Rhine, during Passover week. Jews were often attacked during holidays, but this was a truly horrific case. On this particular week, a Christian child disappeared one morning and hadn't returned the following day. The mother of the child grew frantic and went to her husband, who was a burly drunkard of a blacksmith."

How on earth, Aaron wondered, could he possibly know that her husband was a "burly drunkard of a blacksmith"?

"The blacksmith," said the professor, "trailed by his wife, began walking around the village, asking after his son and rounding up other men. Gradually they formed a sort of mob and went down to the synagogue, where they demanded that the rabbi give back the little boy. The rabbi calmly stood before them and asserted that neither he, nor any of the Jews, knew anything about the disappearance. The more the rabbi insisted, the more belligerent the crowd became.

"Inevitably, the scene turned violent. The townspeople went door to door in the Jewish neighborhood, forcing all the residents into the streets. History records a few incidents of antisemitism in that town, but never anything of this nature. Herding all the Jews together, they marched them down to the Rhine, where there was a type of barge used for transporting goods along the river. The townspeople proceeded to force the Jews onto the boat and inside the cabin. Ignoring the dreadful cries from within, they chained the cabin doors shut and set it on fire. Using poles, they pushed it out into the river and watched as the flames licked up the sides, consuming the boat and everyone in it."

"That's horrifying," murmured Aaron.

"It is. It is terrible. Terrible." The professor hesitated. "But I haven't yet gotten to the point of the story."

Professor Freeman stopped himself. He held up his hand and rolled his eyes upward, lost in thought.

"What?" asked Aaron.

"Let me stop there. I'll tell you the rest, but first let me tell you one other story. Do you know anything about the pogroms?"

"A little bit."

"Good, so you know they were essentially riots against Jews in Tsarist Russia in which thousands and thousands of Jews were viciously murdered," Professor Freeman said with a wave of his hand. "I won't go into the details. I just want to tell you about one specific event that took place in Odessa at the beginning of the nineteenth century.

Odessa, if you don't know, is a port city on the Black Sea in present-day Ukraine. This is another gruesome tale, I'm afraid."

Aaron nodded, in slight disbelief that the professor was straying further and further from the initial purpose of the meeting, and yet too intrigued to be bothered.

"Living in Odessa at that time was a certain Tsarist official by the name of Vladimir Shevchenko, known simply as Sheva. Notorious throughout the empire for his slipperiness and cruelty, he was feared by many and imitated by others. On the side, he ran a shipping business, which had made him a very rich man. His wealth was far greater than that of an average official in the Russian empire. But he was also a very greedy and vindictive man. He would go to any lengths to snuff out his competition.

"One of Sheva's competitors was a Greek Jew who had immigrated to Odessa as a teenager. He had started out as a waterfront worker, but through sheer hard work and an ounce of guile he had built a lucrative shipping business. Of course, it was tiny compared to Sheva's massive enterprise. Still, Sheva couldn't stand to have an upstart Jewish immigrant succeed in siphoning off even a dime from his business. One night, Sheva went to two of his dockworkers and made an arrangement. He gave them the location of a house in a Jewish neighborhood and left the rest to them.

"The following week, the dockworkers rounded up a crowd of ruffians and began what would become one of the biggest pogroms the city of Odessa ever witnessed, centered on the Jewish neighborhood of Sheva's shipping rival. Naturally, they burned the Greek immigrant's house to the ground, killing him and his family. That was only a small part of the death and destruction that ensued. Over the course of a week, the mobs killed over a thousand Jews. Houses and businesses were demolished, women raped, children torn limb from limb.

"In the terrifying chaos, the rioters were constantly coming up with new ways to murder as many Jews as they could. They would line them up and shoot them or pack them inside of carriages and burn them. In one very macabre scene—and this is what I want to tell you about—they marched dozens of Jews to a bell tower and threw them out one by one. As the bodies splattered, men below would pull them away to clear the cobblestones for the next falling body."

At this, Aaron's face had contorted to such a degree that Professor Freeman felt the need to cut short the grisly description.

"I'm sorry," the professor said. "I can stop if this is too much."

"No, no. I want to hear it."

"Are you sure?"

"I'm sure."

"Okay. Well, I apologize for the brutality of what I'm telling you, but it is necessary for understanding the whole story. I'm just getting to the important part."

The professor hesitated, and Aaron shifted forward, hanging on his words.

"But first let's go back," said the professor. "I'm sure you're still curious about the other story. Tell me, what would you guess happened on the river that day?"

Aaron collapsed back in his chair, unprepared for the question. He crossed his arms and gathered his thoughts.

"You mean about the boat on the Rhine?"

"Right."

"I don't know. It doesn't seem like anyone could have survived."

"But?"

"Did someone survive?"

Professor Freeman sighed with a smirk.

"Here is what happened that day. Once the river had completely engulfed the burning boat, the townspeople went back to their houses. Some men got together and drank; others retired to their homes, distressed over what they had done. The mother whose son had disappeared went back to her home in tears. When she stepped through the door, she nearly fainted. Sitting at the table like an apparition was her son! He had his leg propped up on a chair. His older sister was wiping his shin down with a wet cloth. The boy looked up at his mother sheepishly, knowing he would face her wrath.

"Later on that night, the son explained what had happened. He had gone a long way up the river exploring on his own and had fallen among the rocks, injuring his leg. He had limped some of the way back before nightfall, at which point he had made a bed for himself amidst the trees at the side of the river. Waking there the next morning, he had slowly hobbled back to the village, taking the whole day to return.

"After a moment of shock, the mother ran from the doorway across the room and grabbed the boy by the shoulders and shook him, screaming and demanding to know where he had been. She collapsed on him in tears. But before he could explain himself, the house went silent. They heard a commotion out in the street. The mother went back to the door. Her son limped after her with the help of the daughter.

"The street was lined with townspeople, who had come out of their houses and their shops and their pubs. All eyes were fixed on a haunting, solitary figure making his way through the center of the road. The people of the town watched in silent horror, sure they were seeing a ghost. They were certain the man they saw—a man they knew as a holy man among the Jews—had been on the boat. One of the townspeople had actually looked into his eyes as they locked the cabin and set the boat aflame.

"The holy man walked through the road slowly, peacefully, glancing neither to his left nor to his right; he drifted along, not sneering at any of the people or looking around accusingly. He gazed straight ahead with deep, penetrating eyes. But when he came to the house of the woman and her son, he abruptly stopped. He turned and took a step toward the boy, who was leaning up against the house with his injured leg lifted. Reaching out, the holy man gently placed his hand on the boy's head. Then he walked out of the village, never to return."

The professor raised his eyebrows and smiled inquisitively at Aaron.

"Was he on the boat, then?" Aaron asked.

Professor Freeman shrugged.

"What happened to him after that?"

"Let me tell you the rest of the other story, about that day in Odessa."

Aaron accepted with a nod, realizing he had again crept all the way forward in his chair.

"It was an overcast day, and a mist had settled over the entire city. I assume you've never been to Odessa?"

Aaron shook his head.

"Think of Boston. Think of the worst fog on the coast. That is how Odessa can be, only much more extreme. I was there several years ago on a Fulbright, and we had four days of fog that blanketed the whole place. You couldn't see a few feet in front of your face. That is what you must imagine. It was a day like that.

"As I was telling you, these barbarians were forcing their victims one by one up to the bell tower and down to their death. Some went willingly, woefully accepting their fate. Those who struggled were stabbed or were wrestled and thrown. When nearly half the Jews had fallen to their death, a man came forward, calmly stepping out of the line. The rioters stood back, momentarily stunned by the serene, almost majestic demeanor of this man. Quiet and composed, he stepped up onto the stones of the belfry. With a little hop, he soared out of the window down to the cobblestone square.

"The rioters looked out after him, but the man quickly disappeared in the fog—falling to his death, they supposed. The men at the bottom of the tower, who were pulling away bodies one by one, heard a softer noise than the previous thuds. They stepped through the fog and laid hands on the man. They were baffled. Where had this man come from, suddenly appearing where the bodies were splattering? Not giving it much thought, they jostled the man back up to the tower.

"The man once more joined the group of Odessan Jews awaiting their execution, as calm as he had been before. When the men in the belfry saw him again, they were astonished. They stared at the man in disbelief; they had watched him leap from the belfry with their own eyes. The man again came forward peacefully, just as he had the first time, and stepped out of the tower, into the fog.

"Down below in the cobblestone square, the men in the crowd at the bottom heard the same sort of gentle landing. They stepped out into the mist, feeling their way with outstretched arms. Trembling, they came upon this man, who stood where he had descended, unscathed. You can imagine their shock—their horror! Two of the men took hold of him lightly, now almost afraid to touch him, and walked him over to the crowd of rioters, where they detained him.

"But Ukrainians are a stubborn people," said Professor Freeman. "When all the other Jews had fallen or been pushed from the tower, one of the leaders of the mob commanded two of the brawnier men to take this mysterious man back up to the tower and hurl him out, once and for all. The two men, unwilling to treat this man roughly, guided him up the winding wooden staircase to the belfry, barely touching him.

They stood at the edge, holding him by the arms, and called out down below. Then they let go and the man floated down, disappearing into the fog.

"They waited. They heard nothing. They waited. Another moment passed. A voice called up to the tower through the mist. Had they thrown the man down? One of the brawny men in the belfry called down in the affirmative. Again, silence. The men down below could not find the man. They hadn't even heard a soft landing the way they had before. The man was gone. He had simply vanished in the mist.

"As the men down below searched the foggy square, murmuring to each other in wonderment, a sudden splattering thud froze them. Another body had fallen from the tower. Getting over their shock, they rushed to the sound and found the corpse."

"What?" said Aaron. "Who was it?"

"What they found," the professor enunciated, "was the body of one of the men who had ushered this mysterious man to the top of the tower. Overwhelmed by terror and guilt, he had thrown himself from the belfry to his death."

Aaron's eyes bulged and his lips parted. The professor looked back at Aaron, waiting for his reaction.

"I don't understand," said Aaron. "What happened to the man?"

"He disappeared."

"What do you mean? Is it true?"

"I don't know," said Professor Freeman. "Do you believe it's true?"

"It obviously seems a little farfetched."

"To some people, miracles don't exist. There is nothing at all you can say or do to change their mind. Are you one of those people?"

"I wouldn't say that."

"What would you say?"

Aaron pondered the question, and in the meantime the professor's phone lit up.

"I'm sorry, I have to take this."

The professor noisily screeched out his chair and darted away with the phone up to his ear. He returned a moment later and hurriedly began collecting his things.

"I have to go."

"Wait," said Aaron. "I still don't understand what it all means."

"I'm sorry, it's very important. We'll have to do it another time."

"What about the Bible story?"

Professor Freeman stopped, the color leaving his cheeks.

"Could we meet tomorrow morning?" Aaron asked.

"Tomorrow morning?" protested the professor. "It's Saturday!"

"So?"

"Fine. Fine. I can do late morning."

Aaron nodded eagerly.

"I'll see you here tomorrow at eleven."

Chapter Three

Holy Man

The next day, Aaron arrived at the café a few minutes early. At quarter after eleven, Professor Freeman strolled in looking slightly bedraggled. He got a coffee and brought it over to the table, sitting down with a sigh.

"Good morning," Aaron ventured.

"Good morning."

Aaron put down his phone, but the professor waved him off.

"No, no. I need a moment."

Professor Freeman stared out the window in a stupor. He delicately sipped his coffee while Aaron scrolled through his phone to keep himself occupied.

"You'll notice I don't teach any morning classes."

"Right," said Aaron.

"You know, this is good," the professor said. "Getting together like this—this is important. It's a shame the way collegiality on campuses has disappeared. Meetings like this used to be much more common. In the past, professors and students had real relationships. It truly is a shame. When I was at Princeton, I developed friendships with several of my professors. It was the same at Dartmouth and Harvard, I should add."

Aaron smiled on one side of his mouth.

"We would get meals together, even get drinks together—it was very different then. But it was at Princeton where I probably had the best relationships with my professors. My advisor there was the legendary Montgomery Lewis."

Professor Freeman paused, allowing the name to make an impression. Aaron tardily widened his eyes and bobbled his head.

"In any case, one Saturday morning, Monty phoned me, which he very rarely did. 'There's a fascinating person on campus today,' he told me. 'You must come meet him.' That was all he said. I agreed, naturally, and early that afternoon I met up with Monty. Together we walked over to another professor's office.

"When we got there, we found three professors sitting in a dim room in a semicircle. It was very eerie. Monty and I slipped in, making as little of a disturbance as possible, and sat down on a wooden bench behind the three professors. I couldn't see the faces of the professors, but I later learned they were three of the most renowned professors at Princeton. In fact, Monty whispered to me that one of them was Marcus Clifton, who is of course world-famous for his theory on divergent ideation—the Clifton Hypothesis. But that's neither here nor there."

Aaron nodded and shrugged.

"Across from these three eminent professors, with his back to the windows, sat a man. I could only see the shape of him at first. He was shrouded in shadows against the light coming in through the stained-glass windows. But I could feel his presence immediately. And I could see his eyes. I can still see his eyes; I will never forget them. They were flashing and brilliant and deep and piercing—otherworldly.

"The room briefly went silent when we came in, and then the man resumed talking. He spoke slowly and rhythmically. He had the worn voice of a very old man, somewhat high-pitched. At the same time his voice was strong and confident, and even soothing in a way. It's difficult to describe. His words were enlightening and assuring. In his presence you felt at peace. It was impossible to doubt him.

"He regaled us with story after story. And he was an absolute encyclopedia. It was unlike anything I've ever come across, and, as you might expect, I've come across some wonderfully brilliant minds over the course of my career. This man knew the last two thousand years of human history as if they had happened yesterday, as if he had lived through them. The breadth and depth of his knowledge was astounding. It didn't seem humanly possible. From time to time one of the professors would respectfully ask him a question related to his stories, and he would be able to provide obscure facts, all verifiable. Trust me! I went back and verified many of them.

"The strange thing was, while it was impossible not to believe him, all his stories were—well—unbelievable. You see it was he who told me those tales I told you, about the boat on the Rhine and the tower in Odessa. Those were perhaps the most memorable, but there were many more. He told of persecutions in Roman times; he told of a massacre in India; there was a little-known event in Morocco in which the Spanish Inquisition burned hundreds of Jews at the stake.

"Of course, one of the Jews would not burn at the stake.

"Probably the most bizarre story he told us took place in Kentucky during the American Civil War. At some point, Ulysses S. Grant gave an order to expel Jews from a particular area. I looked it up; it really did happen. The order never went through, but some of his soldiers attacked the local Jewish population, lynching several of them.

"But one of the Jews, as you might guess, simply would not hang.

"However, the stories themselves, as impossible as they seemed, were not what was so unbelievable. What we couldn't make sense of was that he claimed to have been present at all these events. He claimed to have spent decades in all corners of the globe; he claimed to have studied at every major university over the centuries; he claimed to have been involved in almost every major historical event in some way or another. And there was no way of disproving him. He could answer every question.

"Even more unbelievably—and this is what is staggering—he didn't just claim to have been a witness to all these persecutions. It was more than that. He claimed to be the survivor! He was the man in Kentucky who wouldn't hang; he was the man in Morocco who wouldn't burn at the stake; he was the man in Odessa who disappeared in the fog; he was the man in the boat on the Rhine who came forth from the river!"

Professor Freeman went silent, his hands folded on the table in front of him. Aaron sat dumbly, his elbow on the table and his palm covering his mouth.

"As I'm sure you have put together," the professor said, "this is the Holocaust survivor I mentioned in class a couple of weeks ago. According to his story, he was the scourge of the Nazis, their absolute nemesis. Over and over the Nazis tried to kill him and he simply would not die. He was imprisoned in almost every camp at one time or another. He started out at Dachau, but they soon got rid of him. They couldn't stand him. They transported him to Treblinka in Poland, where they marched him into the gas chambers. You see, they thought he was a frail old man. How right they were and how wrong they were!"

Professor Freeman began to laugh, and then caught himself, realizing he was getting carried away with the story.

"I apologize," he said. "I don't mean to treat this subject lightly. I know that your grandfather was a Holocaust survivor, but this story is truly incredible. You must hear it."

"It's okay," said Aaron. "I understand."

"So as soon as he got to Treblinka," Professor Freeman said, striking a more somber tone, "they sent him to the gas chambers. Of course, when they opened the doors to clear out the bodies, he walked out, much as he had walked out of the town next to the Rhine. They thought there must have been some error, so they beat him viciously and sent him back to the gas chambers. Yet again, he emerged, filling the guards with fright.

"They dragged him away and beat him and, although he suffered under their blows, he didn't crumple. Several guards put him against a wall and shot at him, but the bullets seemed to dodge him, scattering all around him. One guard held a pistol to his head, and it wouldn't fire. They changed guns and that one wouldn't fire. At last, they backed away, dumbfounded, trembling with fear. They refused to go near him again. As soon as they possibly could, they shipped him out to another camp.

"The same sorts of things happened elsewhere. Obviously it wasn't long before he became notorious. They sent him from camp to camp—from Belzek to Sobibor, from Auschwitz to Mauthausen. None of them wanted him. In fact, they were terrified of him. At one camp they were so desperate to get rid of him that they provided him a chauffeured car to another camp! I can still remember the way he quietly chuckled and his eyes twinkled when he told us that."

Aaron's awe quickly turned to disgust. Thoughts of Professor Freeman's reputation as a fraud returned to him. This seemed to be unfolding into a bad joke. How could the professor talk such nonsense? How could he discuss something so serious with such sickening irreverence? Aaron's revulsion showed on his face, causing Professor Freeman to hesitate.

"Again," the professor said, "I'm sorry. This probably sounds terribly disrespectful."

"It does a little bit, yeah," said Aaron.

"I understand completely. I am certain that the thoughts that are passing through your mind are some of the very same thoughts that passed through my mind when I heard this man speak. But there is still more to the story. Please be patient."

Aaron leaned back in his chair and crossed his arms.

"As I was saying, I too was offended on some level when I heard these stories. I felt both disturbed and confused—confused because the man was clearly special. He was no raving lunatic, yelling in the streets. He may have been insane, but there was something deeply spiritual about him. Even though it went against all logic, he appeared to be telling the truth.

"Walking back to my apartment that day, I thought of something. I ran home to get my Polaroid camera and raced back to the office. The office was empty. The professors and this mysterious man had left. I ran down the hallway, frantically searching for them. From a window, I saw down into the courtyard. Below, making their way through a colonnade, was the man and two of the professors. I sprinted back down the hallway and down the stairs. I burst out into the courtyard, and they all looked in my direction. I was ashamed, but I couldn't be deterred. As politely as I could, I approached the man to ask if I could take a picture of him—ignoring the professors, who were embarrassed and annoyed. The man didn't say anything; he just made one long nod. I took the picture and thanked him and was off.

"For years I did nothing with the photo. I kept it in my files somewhere, waiting for an opportunity to use it. In the meantime, I did as much research as I could about the stories. The historical details available were sparse, but none of them contradicted the stories. I concluded that in all likelihood he was a madman and a genius. He must have memorized all the facts and then carefully constructed these colorful tales. For what purpose, I couldn't say. Anyway, as you can tell, the experience stayed with me.

"Then my opportunity to use the photo came. I was in Germany on a grant one summer. Little did the grant board know how I spent my last three weeks! Through a great deal of diligence and some luck, I managed to track down the addresses for a handful of former Nazi soldiers who had worked at the camps. Unfortunately, most of the addresses were wrong; in other cases, the men had passed away or they refused to see me. It took several days of travelling on trains and knocking on doors before I finally found someone, at a little cottage outside of Mainz. A plump, middle-aged woman came to the door. She brought me to her ancient father, who sat hunched over in a chair at a window, watching the wind sweep across the farm fields.

"I tried to question him for quite a while, but he gave very terse and unhelpful answers. Getting nowhere, I decided to show him the photograph. I opened up my leather satchel on my lap and pulled out the old Polaroid. He wouldn't take it in his hand, so I held it up in front of his eyes. It took a moment for him to focus his vision, but as soon as he did, a storm passed over him. He completely shut down. He went into a sort of catatonic state. I went to find his daughter. She knelt down and tried to coax him, and still he didn't come out of his spell. She told me that sometimes he got like that and showed me to the door.

"The next man I found was younger and more vigorous. He was probably in his seventies, but he was fit and strong. He was a bachelor, living alone in a grubby little apartment in Berlin. He was the unapologetic sort, defensive and combative. They were acting under orders, he repeated over and over, no matter what I asked him. I tried to make simple conversation with him, but he would challenge me before I could even finish my sentences. When I brought up the stories from the camps, he denied them angrily, calling them ridiculous. At last, I showed him the photo. He took one look at it and exploded, screaming at me to get out of his house. He stood up violently and thrust my satchel into my chest and pushed me to the door. It was really a little frightening. As you can see, I'm not such a large man.

"Then, on the day before I left, I got lucky one more time, at a large, modern house in the suburbs of Berlin. This last man was obviously more stable than the other two. He was happily married and had pictures of his children and grandchildren all over his impressive home. We talked for a long time, and he showed clear remorse for all that had happened and his part in it, even breaking down in tears at one point.

"With him I felt comfortable enough to tell the whole story of my strange encounter with the man at Princeton. I showed him the picture, but he didn't recognize it at all. Throughout the story, he shook his head. It seems absurd, he kept muttering. But when I got to the stories from the Nazi camps, his demeanor changed. He listened carefully and thoughtfully.

"When I finished, he spoke measuredly, almost apologetically. 'Rumors about events like that were always floating around the camps,' he explained, 'rumors of ghosts and holy men. Many of those stories sound familiar to me. I never believed any of them. It was the most awful thing the Nazis were doing, and I think some men began to lose touch with reality. However,' he said, 'I must admit that there was one man in particular that the guards always talked about. I never believed any of it, but I suppose that could be the man.'"

Professor Freeman went silent.

"Then what happened?" pressed Aaron.

"Well, that was it. I had to leave Germany the next day."

"So you never learned anything more?"

"Not exactly."

"What do you mean?"

"There is one other thing I haven't told you."

"What?"

"My father, like your grandfather, was a Holocaust survivor. He died a few years ago."

"I'm sorry."

"Before he died, though," said Professor Freeman, "I went to see him one day in the hospital. At the time, he was at Mount Sinai in New York and was suffering terribly. It was difficult to see—a man who had already suffered so much. Anyway, one day I went to him—at that point he hadn't said anything in nearly a year—and I showed him the picture of the man I had met at Princeton. When I brought the Polaroid up to his eyes, a certain peace came over him. I could feel it. I can't explain it, but I could feel it. Then he coughed, and it looked as though he was trying to say something. I came close to his face, and he sighed—the word barely rising above his breath—'*kodesh*.'"

Professor Freeman waited, looking into Aaron's eyes.

"Do you know what *kodesh* means?" he asked.

Aaron nodded, staring back.

"Holy man," Professor Freeman whispered.

Aaron sat motionless, distracted by his thoughts, and utterly overwhelmed. Thanking the professor, he walked out of the coffee shop in a daze, leaving the professor alone at the table.

Chapter Four

A Different Holocaust Survivor

Over the weekend, Aaron could not stop thinking about the stories. Allowing his mind to wander, he visualized this holy man in the concentration camps. He imagined this same man suffering and surviving for centuries and centuries. The idea was captivating, and also moving. That night he couldn't sleep, and when he dozed, he dreamt of pogroms and concentration camps.

The next morning, the magic wore off. Recovering from his fascination, Aaron again considered what he had heard. The whole thing defied logic; it could not exist in the reality he knew. Still, unless Professor Freeman was lying through his teeth, parts of it were difficult to explain. This man must have existed, because he saw him at Princeton, and he must have been in the Nazi camps, or else the picture would have meant nothing.

The more he tried to imagine this holy man in the concentration camps, the more Aaron reflected on his grandfather, who had his own incredible tales of survival. Even the most banal details about daily life in the camps were almost impossible to fathom. The idea that human beings could treat other human beings that way was entirely foreign to his generation. Aaron knew he was fortunate to have a grandfather who had experienced the camps. In his childhood home, sleeping in the room next to his was a living representative of the horrors of Nazi Germany. Grandpa Moshe was walking proof of the atrocities that had taken place. Without that, Aaron could understand how the Holocaust could seem impossible.

The funny thing was that Grandpa Moshe himself, in a way, made the Holocaust seem impossible. Aaron had wondered from the time he was a child how a person who had been through so much could be so silly. As soon as Aaron was old enough to hear the stories, he had asked his mother a very reasonable question.

"Mom," he had said, "why is Grandpa Moshe so happy?"

His mother had laughed, but Aaron was earnest.

"Why are you laughing?" he had asked.

"Grandpa Moshe is happy," she had said, "because he is alive."

That was true, of course, but the reality was more complicated. Grandpa Moshe was happy and silly because Grandpa Moshe was a happy and silly person, and nothing was going to change that. Nothing could break that, not even a Nazi concentration camp. That was the biggest lesson Aaron had learned from his grandfather. The Nazis could take away everything, and they did, but they couldn't take away the thing that made a person a person. They couldn't reach the glowing core deep inside of each individual. The spirit, the soul—whatever you wanted to call it—they couldn't touch it.

That didn't mean that the concentration camps didn't change a person. On the contrary, not one person survived as the same person. The personality might remain the same, but the person changed. Aaron found his grandfather's many levels of identity fascinating. As a child, Aaron only saw the playful old man, full of tricks and teasing. When he got older, he saw the man who could not bear to get out of bed on certain days, whose pain of memory could become a physical pain, a debilitating weakness. He saw the man who would sit alone in a room for hours and hours, staring out into the back yard, his eyes gleaming with tears that would not fall.

There were more layers, too. Grandpa Moshe was not the stereotypical melancholy old man who could only bear to laugh when he was laughing with children. He didn't indulge in childish games to escape the dire reality of adulthood. He could talk to anyone, on any level, and he had a sharp wit. He loved to frolic, as Aaron's mother would sometimes put it. And she did get sick of it at times.

Grandpa Moshe would groan and elbow Aaron when she brought out a dish of leftovers. "Looks like we've got camp food tonight," he would say under his breath.

Aaron's mother was not at all entertained. She would beat down the metal serving spoon with a little extra force on his porcelain plate. She had plenty of reason to be impatient with him. After all, she did everything for him, even if she wouldn't have it any other way.

When he retired from his professorship, as early as he could "—Contrary to what you may have heard, work will not set you free" was another one of his uncomfortable concentration camp jokes that no one knew exactly what to do with—Aaron's mother insisted that he live with them. He told her she didn't need to worry about him. He said he would be happy living on his own, or even going to one of those "elderly concentration camps," also known as nursing homes. In fact, at times he could not stop making jokes about the camps, which really ruffled his daughter's feathers, particularly given she was a professor of Jewish Studies. Of course, he never made those kinds of jokes outside of the family.

Aaron's mother would not hear of his spending the rest of his days alone, after all the loss he had experienced. He had lost his whole family in the Holocaust. He had watched the Nazis drag away his young wife and his toddler. For years, he searched for them, refusing to break his commitment to his wife. He wrote everyone he knew, hoping that somehow his family had survived. No one could tell him what had happened. After ten years in America, he saved enough money to go back to look for them. Finally, he gave up hope. Soon after that, he married

Aaron's grandmother, another Polish Jew. But he had lost her, too. She died of lung cancer before Aaron was born. By the time Grandpa Moshe reached retirement age, he was alone again.

Aaron's mother could not bear to think of him all on his own in some depressing apartment in New Jersey, frittering away his days at the cheap diner around the corner. She told him he didn't have a choice. And, truthfully, she also wanted him in the house for her own reasons, namely for Aaron's sake. She wanted her father to be an intrinsic part of Aaron's upbringing, and she wanted Aaron to be exposed to all that her father represented. And, just as importantly, or perhaps more importantly, she wanted Aaron to have a male figure in his life. Her husband was gone before Aaron was born.

In the end, living with his daughter turned out to be a perfect situation for Grandpa Moshe. He had access to all the reading and research he wanted in the Boston area. He quickly became a known figure at his daughter's university. He gave guest lectures from time to time, and they gave him his own shared office space in the library for his research. He also had plenty of time and money to travel, given that his daughter refused to accept rent payments. He was regularly on the road, which could be a welcome change for his daughter.

Grandpa Moshe had been in the house from as far back as Aaron could remember. He took Aaron to the playground; he walked him to school and picked him up after school. Most people assumed he was Aaron's father, and at least early on, he could easily pass for an older father. For a long time, even most of Aaron's friends thought he was his father. Eventually, they all learned who he was, and they revered him. They treated him with the utmost respect, going quiet any time he appeared. His friends' parents likewise attended to him as he if was Moses himself. He always put them at ease with a kind word or got the kids laughing with a wisecrack.

Grandpa Moshe genuinely appreciated the veneration. He also thought it could verge on ridiculous. Certain people were over the top. Aaron's high school history teacher was one of them. He had invited Grandpa Moshe to come into class during the unit on the Second World War. Any time Aaron's classmates tried to ask an interesting question, the teacher chastised them and told them they were being inappropriate.

"Next time he should just put me inside a glass case and charge admission," Grandpa Moshe had said when they got in the car after.

He firmly held that Holocaust survivors should be more than Holocaust survivors. He knew survivors who had spent the rest of their days talking of nothing else. In a sense, they put themselves inside a glass case, and that was the worst thing they could do. Of course, every person had a different life to lead, and he was always careful not to demean others. At the same time, he believed that surviving the Holocaust came with a mission to live a full life, to make the most of every minute on earth.

Grandpa Moshe was proud to say that he had been a professor of psychology. He hadn't devoted his life to studying the Torah or Jewish culture or Twentieth Century history simply because the Nazis had tried to kill him off. No, he had survived, and so he would go on to do whatever he wanted to do. He had begun studying psychology before the war, and he would continue to study psychology after the war. The Nazis could not destroy who he was. That was the idea that always came back around with Grandpa Moshe.

As Aaron reflected on his grandfather, he suddenly realized what he had to do. He immediately sent an email to Professor Freeman.

Chapter Five

A Visit with Grandpa Moshe

"Guard this with your life," said Professor Freeman.

"I'll have it back to you first thing on Monday," said Aaron.

The professor handed over an envelope with a button-and-string fastener. Aaron carefully slotted it in the front of his backpack and zipped it up. He nodded and left.

"No thumb prints," called the professor.

Aaron went straight to his car and unzipped his backpack. He delicately opened the envelope and slipped out the Polaroid picture. A chill ran up his spine. His heart immediately began to thump in his chest. The man was exactly as Professor Freeman had described. He had a piercing gaze. He was magisterial. His authority emanated from the photograph. He was also ghoulish, in a way. The man was a ghost. Aaron shook his head free and slid the picture back into the envelope.

Aaron spent the entire drive back to Boston with the picture fixed in his head. He could think of nothing else. The mysterious man was real to him in a way he hadn't been before. And still, the stories were too fantastical to be true. He hoped that somehow his grandfather would be able to make sense of it all. If Professor Freeman's father had recognized the person in the picture, Grandpa Moshe might recognize him, as well. Maybe his own grandfather had met this mysterious man. The thought made his hair stand up.

Aaron's mother opened the door.

"Aaron! What are you doing here?"

She threw herself at her son, wrapping her arms around his neck.

"Hi, mom."

"I'm so happy to see you," she said. "Your grandfather has been driving me crazy."

"Oh. Great."

"He's in his chair. I'm sorry. I've got to keep working. I've got grades due."

Aaron's mother squeezed him one more time and jogged upstairs. Aaron set his backpack down and poked his head around the corner to the living room. Grandpa Moshe was sitting in his armchair, facing out on the back yard as the sun fell.

"Grandpa?"

Grandpa Moshe stirred, as if waking from a nap. He looked up awkwardly over the back of his chair.

"Aaron? Is that you?"

"Yeah, it's me. I'm back for the weekend."

"Come over here and give me a hug."

Aaron bent over to hug his grandfather where he sat. He seemed more fragile than he had remembered. He placed a weak hand on Aaron's back when he hugged him.

"You doing okay?"

"Oh, yeah. Of course," said Grandpa Moshe.

Aaron nodded.

"I may be old, but I'm still the best-looking Jew I know. No offense."

"None taken, Grandpa."

"I've got good news, too."

"Oh, yeah?"

"Yeah, I was reading the obituaries this morning and guess what?"

"What?"

"I'm not dead yet."

"You're right," Aaron said with a shrug. "Great news."

"Where's Miriam? Where'd your mother go?"

"She went upstairs. She said she had to work."

"Always working."

Grandpa Moshe livened up. After a cup of tea, he showed Aaron the calisthenics routine he had gotten into, which involved all sorts of spinning around and body contortions, some of which seemed fairly difficult. Aaron was impressed.

"They're called Tibetan Rites," Grandpa Moshe explained. "Only rights they got, last I checked. Let's see if you can do them."

Aaron was no athlete. He did his best to imitate his grandfather, but some of the exercises were not at all easy. He climbed up off the floor with a huff, defeated. Grandpa Moshe patted him on the shoulder.

"You'll get there some day. You got fifty years to practice."

They ordered food for dinner. Aaron's mother rushed back downstairs when the doorbell rang. She paid the deliveryman and yelled for Aaron and Grandpa Moshe as she swerved into the dining room with the food. She was frantically setting the table when Aaron appeared in the dining room.

"Do you need help?"

"Nope, I'm fine. I just have more work to do."

"Are you sure? I can set the table."

"I can do it. It's almost done."

Aaron stood near the wall of the dining room, staying out of the way. His mother darted back into the kitchen and reappeared a moment later with glasses and a pitcher of filtered water. Grandpa Moshe arrived as she was setting the glasses around the small table.

"And here comes Miriam," he said, pretending to hold a microphone to his mouth. "She's coming down the back stretch with a head of steam. Look at the way she's taking that outside corner. And she's taken the lead! No one can catch her now. She's going, she's going . . ."

Aaron chuckled quietly. Miriam stopped and put her hands on her hips.

"Seriously?" she said. "That's what you have to say?"

"I'm just kidding, Miriam. Come on."

"You know, I don't have time for this. Really and truly. I don't."

"Mom, he was just kidding."

"Don't you start," she said.

They all sat down to the meal. Miriam opened the Styrofoam containers. Leaning over the table, she spooned out helpings onto the three plates.

"I'm telling you," she said, "these are microaggressions. It's a real thing. My students told me about them."

"Mom, it was a joke," said Aaron.

"You know, I'm keeping a record of this stuff."

"Oh, yeah. We know," said Grandpa Moshe.

"No, no. I'm serious. I have a notebook upstairs. You better be careful. I'm collecting all these little microaggressions against me."

"Oh, that's what you've been working on! That's why you're so busy all the time."

"Yep, that's right. That's another one. Keep 'em coming. As soon as that notebook is all full, I'm going to the dean."

"Yeah, and what's he going to do?"

"He's going to take away your little office space that you love so much."

"Oh, no, not my little office space that I share with four other people."

"Yep, that one. He's going to take it away."

"Where would I read the newspaper in the afternoon?"

"You'll just have to figure that out."

Finally, Miriam allowed herself to smirk, and they all laughed together as they began to eat. After a few minutes, she held up her fork and shook it at the air.

"But I'm serious. You better stop with those microaggressions."

"Yeah, yeah, yeah," said Grandpa Moshe.

Miriam ate quickly and hurried back upstairs. Grandpa Moshe returned to the living room as Aaron cleared the table and put the leftovers in the refrigerator. Grandpa Moshe told him where his mother had started keeping her secret chocolate supply, in the back corner of the small cupboard above the stove.

"She thinks I can't get up there," he said as he disappeared into the other room.

Aaron brought his grandfather a cup of instant coffee with the chocolate. They sat down in front of the television to watch a basketball game. They talked sports for a while, catching up on the last couple months of the season. Grandpa Moshe knew his stuff. He had an incredible knowledge of sports history, but he also stayed on top of all the current players and trends. He was a junky.

"You can't guard him," he said. "He's a match-up nightmare."

Aaron nodded. Most of his love for sports derived purely from the time he spent with his grandfather in front of the television throughout his childhood. He would never have been a sports fan if not for him.

"Watch this, here we go," said Grandpa Moshe. "They set a pick, they get the switch, and bang, it's over. It's like clockwork. They need a timeout."

"Yeah."

"Yep, see. They called a timeout."

The game went to commercial, and Aaron went to the front hall to get his backpack. He sat back down with the envelope in his lap.

"What do you have there?" asked Grandpa Moshe.

"There's something I want to ask you about."

"Yeah?"

"Yeah, its actually the reason I came home this weekend."

"Oh, no. What is this about?"

"It's not anything bad," said Aaron. "It's just something strange."

Grandpa Moshe looked at his grandson. He slowly took the controller from his knee and clicked off the television.

"I'm not exactly sure where to start, but I thought I needed to talk to you. I have this professor. I don't know if I trust him completely or not. He seems sort of like a joker. He's full of all kinds of crazy stories."

"Yeah, I know the type."

"Right."

"What's his name? No, don't tell me. I don't want to know."

"Anyway, I decided I would meet with him outside of class because he said he had some fascinating story about a Holocaust survivor."

"Okay. What happened?"

"Well, I met with him. Actually, I met with him a few times."

"Don't tell me you're dating this guy."

"No, no, no, that's not it."

"Okay, good. That would be one for your mom."

"No, nothing like that. It's just that he told me these crazy stories. They're wild. They don't make any sense. It's supernatural stuff. Even saying this out loud, I feel stupid."

"What are they about? Tell me."

"I don't know. Maybe I shouldn't say. I feel stupid."

"No, tell me."

"The stories really don't make any sense. The professor told me all these tales about a mysterious man—a sort of superhuman man, an immortal man. According to the stories, this man has basically been alive forever."

Grandpa Moshe looked away and nodded.

"This man—he was a Jew, or he is a Jew—he lived through persecution after persecution. He lived through medieval crusades against the Jews; he lived through pogroms in Eastern Europe. Obviously, he lived through the Holocaust. This is all according to the professor. It doesn't make sense, right?"

"What do you have there?" said Grandpa Moshe.

"This is the thing that has me confused."

"What is it?"

Aaron stood the envelope up on his lap and hesitated.

"The thing that doesn't add up," said Aaron, "is that the professor claims that he actually met this person. On top of that, he has a picture of him."

"He has a picture of him?"

Aaron dropped the envelope back down onto his lap and unwound the string. He removed the old Polaroid, the picture face down, and handed it to his grandfather, who slowly flipped it over. Aaron waited, sliding forward to the edge of his chair. Grandpa Moshe examined the picture for a moment and raised his head.

"It's him," he said.

"What? Who?"

"It's my old philosophy professor."

Grandpa Moshe broke down in laughter and handed over the photograph. Aaron sank back in his chair.

"I don't know," said Grandpa Moshe. "It's a tall tale. Your professor probably just found an old picture in some curiosity shop some place."

Grandpa Moshe flicked the television back on.

"Yeah, I guess he must just be lying," said Aaron.

"Sorry to say it, but I think that's the case. You can't trust some of these guys."

"I'm usually not that gullible."

"Yeah, I know you're not. Don't worry, Aaron. It happens," said Grandpa Moshe. "But hey, look, we're back in the game. They must have figured out how to play defense."

Grandpa Moshe turned up the volume. They said little after that. Aaron could barely follow the basketball. He felt incredibly stupid. And he was mad. How could he have let Professor Freeman string him along like that? But the stories still seemed so real to him. Midway through the third quarter of the game, Grandpa Moshe abruptly stirred.

"I better get to bed," he said. "I'm not as young as I once was. Let me know who wins."

"Goodnight, Grandpa."

"Goodnight, Aaron."

Chapter Six

Grandpa Moshe's Minor Miracle

Aaron lay in bed on his back, staring up. The full moon spread light and shadow across the ceiling. He hadn't been able to fall asleep. He hadn't even been able to close his eyes. He had hoped that his grandfather would be able to provide resolution, and in a way, he had. But Aaron realized that he had been hoping for something other than resolution. He had, in fact, been hoping for confirmation. He wanted to believe that the stories were true, and part of him could not let go of the possibility that they were true.

Aaron turned onto his side. The distant moon had drifted across the night sky into his view through the window. He was beginning to doze when he heard someone in the hallway. He shifted onto his back and saw that Grandpa Moshe was standing hunched over in the doorway, his face aglow in the moonlight.

"Grandpa?"

"I've never been able to sleep on a full moon," said Grandpa Moshe.

Aaron shuffled in the blankets, pulling himself up into a seated position.

"Mind if I sit down?"

Aaron nodded, and his grandfather lowered himself into the armchair just inside the door, beside the foot of the bed. He pulled the door with him.

"The good thing about being old," he said, "is that you know you're old. You're allowed to take everything slow, which is probably what I should've been doing twenty years ago."

"You seem to be doing pretty well to me."

"Yeah, yeah. Being old isn't as bad as you think. But it sure happens fast. I can still remember when I was your age like it was yesterday."

"Yeah?"

"Oh, yeah. You'll see. It will be the same for you." Grandpa Moshe sighed. "Yeah, I was a student, just like you. The difference was I was married. Can you imagine being married?"

"Not really."

"Well, I bet you wouldn't have minded being married to this woman. She was a special woman. She was the most brilliant woman I've ever known—brilliant in every way. I'm sure there were more beautiful women out there, but not to me. She was the most beautiful.

"Those days of my youth play across my mind like an old film reel. They were the best days I'll ever have. Agata would ride over on her bicycle to meet me in the late afternoon. She was studying history. I think she was the only woman in the history department—smart as a whip. We would ride to a place that looked over the river, a hillside on the outskirts of the town. Sometimes she would bring some little treat for us, a piece of sweet bread or a little cake. We would savor every last bit. She would hold the cake, and break off pieces for us, and I would put both my hands underneath her hands to make sure we didn't lose even the smallest crumb.

"We would sit on the grassy hill, which really wasn't very comfortable with the spiky grass that was there, and watch the sun go down. I never wanted the sun to fall behind the hill because I knew Agata would say she had to go. She would tell me she had to return to her studies, and she would say that I had to return to my studies, too. She would stand up, and I would pull at her fingertips, begging her to sit back down, just for one more minute. The sun had fallen, but the sunset went on. For several minutes we would remain that way. I would hold on desperately to her fingertips, begging her to stay, and she would say she had to leave.

"And that was how they took her away from me. They dragged her away. She held on to our baby daughter, and I held on to her fingertips for as long as I could."

Grandpa Moshe went silent. Aaron was at a loss. He followed Grandpa Moshe's gaze out to the moon, and they both stared at the glowing orb.

"But that was not the last time I saw her," said Grandpa Moshe, his eyes gleaming in the moonlight. "No, there is something I have never told anyone, not even your mother or your grandmother. I did see Agata again."

"You mean in the camps?" asked Aaron.

"No, not in the camps. I saw her later, years later. I don't know if I've ever told you what happened to me after the war. When the Soviets liberated Poland, almost no one was left. Well before the end of the war, the Nazis had killed off most of the Jews in Poland. I was a broken man, a shell of a man. My body was dead. I was only a soul. I was without a home, without a people. I had survived on a shadow of hope. I was no more than the tiny ember on a candle wick after the flame has been blown out.

"All along I had searched for news of Agata. That was one way we got from one day to the next. Every time a new person came into the camps, everyone crowded around them the first chance we had. We pleaded for news, any news at all. In the beginning, I heard that she was sent to another camp. I heard that all the children were gone. They had piled them into the back of huge military trucks. Those children who tried to escape were thrown back into the trucks by their limbs, as if they were ragdolls. They were never seen again.

"But news of Agata quickly dried up. No one could say anything for sure. Many were killed; many died. I could not know if Agata was among the living or the dead. There were 20,000 Jews in Kalisz before the war. And today? None.

"I went back to our town alone. I asked everyone I saw if they could tell me of Agata, or of anyone from my town. I was the only one I knew for sure had survived. The town was decimated, little more than a barracks for the Nazis. They had lived in the most luxurious houses and taken what they wanted. The town was a brothel to them. My own neighborhood was no longer my neighborhood. The Nazis had scarcely touched our streets, but our houses were not empty. When the Nazis had taken the town, the people of the town had taken our homes.

"I stood looking at the houses, as if in a dream, when a van came rumbling down the street toward me. Two men were in the front. The one in the passenger seat waved me down. He said nothing. He pointed to the back of the van with his thumb. The van pulled past me and stopped. In the open back of the van, a dozen men who looked like me, like skeletons, were sitting with their backs against the sides of the van. They didn't move. They looked at me, silent as ghosts. I climbed in beside them, and the van drove on.

"We drove and drove, stopping in towns for scraps of food, finding more men along the way. We drove through the night, all of us too frightened to stop, afraid that we were only dreaming, that we would soon all return to the nightmare we had endured. After days of driving, we turned onto a long dirt road. I was dozing at the time. The man hunched against the wall next to me nudged me. I saw out of the back of the van that on either side of the road were more men who looked like us, walking corpses. They were all going down the same road. We began to wave at them. What else could we do? We waved at them, and they waved. We began to smile, and soon all of us in the back of this van were laughing as we bumped around.

"At the end of the road, the driver turned the van in a circle and stopped to let us off. The two men waved at us, and we went to grasp their hands, to thank them for what they had done. Those two men were saints. They drove straight on, back to Poland to find more men. Every several days, those two men appeared again with another load of survivors. And other men were doing the same all the time.

"We had arrived at the camp set up by the Allies for us. In a way, the camp was a pathetic place. You can imagine, or you've seen pictures. We were a sad sight, and at the same time such a happy sight. We were so overwhelmed with gratitude. No one had much food anywhere in those days, but they had provided food for us. They had tents and cots for us. They had set up a camp not for animals, but for human beings.

"Of course, the first thing I did was ask everyone I could about Agata. I asked the men at the gates who had lists and lists of names. But everyone wanted to see the lists. They told us all to move on. We were all searching, hoping for miracles. And some found miracles. All around the camp, loved ones were reunited with one another. Old friends rediscovered each other. We all told our stories, told what had happened. I kept hoping that I, too, would experience a miracle. The first day passed, and the next. No one could give me any news of Agata."

Grandpa Moshe paused. His brow heavy. Aaron watched him.

"A silence like an abyss," said Grandpa Moshe.

Aaron could think of nothing to say. After another moment, Grandpa Moshe went on.

"When my opportunity came to join the thousands leaving for the United States, after months and months in the camp, I knew I was meant to go. Poland was no longer my home. Europe was not my place. With a heavy heart, I said goodbye to the land where my ancestors had once found refuge. I went in search of a new home, a new life. And I was fortunate. I quickly found a new home and a new life. Very quickly, within only a year, I was able to return to my studies. I was blessed. Many were never able to return to their true work. They became clothes-makers and factory workers. They did whatever jobs they could, and they did them happily.

"I was fortunate. I was not famous or brilliant or anything. I was fortunate. I was blessed. I cannot possibly explain to you the chances. I was alone when I arrived in New York. I lived in a house with several other men, all of us simply trying to make ends meet. I took any opportunity I could during that time. We would gather outside one of the buildings a few blocks away, and people would come by with jobs. Or sometimes, rarely, someone might even come to the house, because they knew we were a house full of men who wanted work.

"One of the jobs I had was delivering clothes for a cleaner. They would send me on foot to deliver cleaned suits and shirts to the successful businessmen in nearby companies. I did that job for some time, and I began to see some of the same people. Often, I would see only secretaries or people at the front desk, but at some of the smaller places I would occasionally deliver the clothes straight to the important people. At that time, just a few blocks away, was a young lawyer who had started his own firm. Everyone said to watch this man, for he was going to rule the city, and eventually he did.

"But at that time, he was starting out, only beginning to grow his firm. He was doing well enough to have his clothes delivered, but not so well to have a big entryway with a doorman to collect the clothes. Every now and then, not always, I would deliver the clothes directly to him. He was a nice man. He was a driven man—always hard at work. But he was a nice man. He wasn't much older than I was.

"The first time I delivered his clothes to him, he asked me my first name, and I told him. He nodded and sent me on my way. The next time, a week or two later, he asked me where I was from. I told him. He nodded and sent me on my way. This went on for many weeks. Each time I saw him, he asked me a single question, until one day he addressed me.

" 'Moshe, who comes from Kalisz, who lives only a few blocks from here in Williamsburg, what do you want to do with your life?'

"I was shocked, and I was afraid to say what I really wanted to do. I feared he would think I was a useless person. But I had nothing else to say, and so I told him.

"I said, 'I want to study psychology.'

"I thought he would laugh at me, but he didn't. He looked up at the ceiling.

" 'Moshe,' he said, 'what is your last name?'

"I told him.

" 'Moshe,' he said, 'I have something to show you.'

"He walked over to a shelf stuffed with books and documents and loose papers. He searched for a moment, and then he slipped out a very small publication, almost a pamphlet. I recognized it immediately. He saw my jaw drop.

" 'I admire your work, Moshe.'

"As I stared in disbelief at the dusty little journal, he explained to me how he had come to have it. The man was from the city nearby to my town—a city called Poznan. He had moved to America with his parents many years before. When he heard of what was happening in Europe, he had gone back to see his grandparents and cousins and anyone else to urge them to leave. As it happened, while in Poznan, this man had picked up one of these publications. He appreciated what I had written, and so he noted my name, and he brought the publication back to America."

"How?" said Aaron. "How did he get it? That's amazing."

"You see, before the war, when I was just a student, my friends and I put out a tiny publication just in our small town. Both Agata and I would go to the university in Poznan once or twice a week to attend lectures or to use the library, and when we did, we would walk around and put one or two of these publications in the coffee shops and other places where students and intellectuals gathered. We did not even live in Poznan, even though we were students at the university. So, you can see what the odds were. But the young lawyer was impressed.

" 'Moshe,' he said to me, 'you must study.'

"And that was it."

"What do you mean?" said Aaron.

"That was it. That was my break. He became my patron. He put me through school. I know it was not easy for him. He was balancing many things, and he was not yet a wealthy man. I owe him everything."

"It's incredible," said Aaron.

"Of course, you've heard that story before," said Grandpa Moshe.

"Not all of it."

"What I'm going to tell you next I know you have not heard. No one has. I have never told a soul."

Chapter Seven

The Search for Agata

"As you know," said Grandpa Moshe. "I completed my undergraduate studies in only a couple years in the city. Back then, especially at my small school, there weren't such strict lines between undergraduate and graduate work. I was simply studying, and studying, and studying. After only a year, I began working as an assistant professor and a tutor for the younger students; a semester after that, I was teaching my own introductory class. With so many young men back from the war, they needed teachers! I did that for a year. I could not find better experience anywhere. My studies, however, were limited. I had to go elsewhere, somewhere bigger, and I was desperate to get out of the city, and so I went out to New Jersey.

"And again, I was very fortunate. I was blessed. Before the war, psychology was barely a department. It was not anywhere near what it is today. After the war came a boom. The military had already been investing huge resources in psychology. As often happens, what started in the military soon spread into the rest of society. A few years after the war, the government began investing huge sums to help grow the study of psychology. And I was there to cash in.

"Within just a few years, I studied and taught my way through a doctorate. With my diploma still hot off the press, I was offered one of two new positions they were adding that year. I'm telling you; it was a boom. In the ten years after the war, I had gone from delivering clothes to delivering lectures. Can you imagine? Remember that I did not even have an undergraduate degree when I arrived in America.

"But in all those ten years, I had never stopped thinking of Agata. I was always dreaming that I would see her again. I came up with all sorts of stories for her. Maybe she had escaped to one of the other Allied countries, or maybe she had even made it to Israel. Naturally, I imagined that she had somehow escaped to America, too, and that she had somehow been able to continue her studies. If me, why not her? I searched for her name at other universities. Everywhere I was, I went to history lectures, dreaming she would be in the crowd. Of course, had she even made it to America, the idea that she had been able to continue her studies was almost impossible. And the idea that she had not found a new husband was even less likely. Still, I hoped.

"In the end, the one thing that seemed least likely of all—so unlikely that I never even imagined it—was what happened."

"I don't understand!" Aaron burst out. "I thought you searched for her."

"Aaron, shh. It is the middle of the night."

"Sorry."

"You'll wake your mother. I searched for her, yes," whispered Grandpa Moshe. "But you are getting ahead.

"I was entering my second year as a professor when I received a letter on official stationery from the law firm of my patron. His name was embossed with gold ink. I was impressed! Years had passed since I had been in New York. When I left to finish my doctorate, I no longer needed his support. My degree was funded. I was teaching. In the meantime, his firm had continued to grow every year. I could tell that the letter had been dictated. Clearly, here was a man with little free time on his hands. The letter may as well have been a telegram. The sentences were not complete. He said he had news. He told me to go see him.

"I did. As soon as I could, I went to the address on the stationery. He had moved from Brooklyn into Manhattan. Now he had a doorman, and a grand entryway, marble and gold. I had to go through layer after layer to see him. Secretaries and young lawyers formed a moat around him, a barrier against people who would waste his time. But when I finally got to his enormous office, he was the same man. He took me by the shoulders and kissed me on the cheek. He pointed to the bookshelves.

" 'You must do something for me,' he said. 'You must sign it.'

"He brought down a slim paperback. I don't know how he got it. A tiny press had published my thesis. My face turned red. I signed the little book for him—my hand was shaking, I was so nervous. I had not sent him the book myself because I was too embarrassed.

" 'And when your next book comes out, you must sign that, too,' he said.

"I only nodded. I owed everything to him. How could he not know that? He must have.

" 'I can't take long,' he went on, 'but I heard about something that might interest you.' He walked all the way around his big desk—a desk like a rampart—and retrieved a piece of paper folded in half. 'I heard from a cousin. A community of survivors is growing in Lodz. Who knows?' he said.

"He didn't say anything else. He didn't want to pry. He didn't know what my circumstances were. He didn't know if I had remarried. Even though he knew my story, he had always been careful not to ask personal questions. He never wanted me to feel that I owed him anything, not even a friendly conversation. I left his office without looking at the piece of paper. In fact, I went all the way back to New Jersey with the piece of paper hidden in my pocket. I was almost afraid for some reason. When I got home, I unfolded the paper on my desk and stared. What had he given me? He had given me a street address in Lodz.

"At that point, I had heard stories of Jews returning to their homes in Europe, to Germany and Austria and Poland—all over. The war was over, but so much was still unsettled, especially for the Jews. Even as I was beginning a new life in America, I was not at ease. I was grateful for my new home, but I was never at home. Many of us who came over from Europe felt that way. We were still looking back. I knew things were astir in Poland, even though it was under Soviet control. Very little information came out, but that information quickly spread among us. Of course, that didn't tell me the meaning of the street address in Lodz. I didn't need anyone to tell me the meaning of the street address is Lodz. I knew immediately.

"I could not realistically leave right away, although I wanted to. I was in the middle of my fall semester, and I did not have enough money saved up. Yet I started to make plans to get to Poland. I had not stopped thinking of Agata, and that year I thought of nothing else. Each day that I worked brought me one day closer to my journey. I still could not know with any certainty that I would find her, or even that she was still alive, and yet I lived every day for her.

"A week after the school year ended. I packed my small suitcase, and I set out. And as you know, it was not so simple as flying into Poland, getting a taxicab from the airport. No, no. I first took a train to New York, where I boarded a boat."

"A boat?"

"That was the way to travel back then. You're seasick? Too bad. The boat was nothing. I arrived in Paris and stayed with a friend I had met during my graduate studies. I had arranged everything, every detail. He helped me get from Paris up through Belgium and to the Netherlands, where I boarded another boat. That was the best way to cross the border into the East—into Soviet Europe. I travelled by boat to Sweden, where there was a man who could get me safely to Poland. Perhaps there was an easier way, but I would not take any risks. I joined a crew of fishermen in the Baltic Sea, and they brought me over to Gdansk. I stayed with a relative of one of my colleagues, another survivor. After two days, he drove us to Lodz.

"So, you see, I searched for her," said Grandpa Moshe. "And that is where I have always ended the story. You may know of my voyage to France, and of my journey into Poland. But that is not where the story ends. I not only searched for her."

"You found her."

"I found her."

"She was at the address?"

"She was at the address."

"Was she married?"

"No. It was not that simple. If only it had been that simple."

"What happened?"

"When we arrived in Lodz, we stayed with other relatives. They were part of a new founding of the Jewish community after the war. The first night, they told us stories of hope, of what had been going on. Jews from all over Poland who had survived the camps were starting over in Lodz. Many of them had gone home to their towns to find what I had found, that their homes were as good as gone. Even those who had lived in Lodz felt they were no longer in the same place. But they were beginning again, with the dream of a new home, a transformation.

"I was too afraid to show the address to my hosts. I did not want them to give me whatever terrible news there might be. I wanted to see the house, to find out for myself what was there. The next morning, I set out alone through the streets of the new Jewish neighborhood. The day was bright, and the people were full of energy, and yet I had a certain ache as I walked past the little shops and the market. The sorrow was not gone. The hope of a new life could not cover over what had happened.

"I easily found the street, which was a quiet, narrow road away from the bustle. I did not want to go to the door. I dreaded the possibility that Agata would answer with a child in her arms, or a wary man with a heavy brow would crack open the door. Instead, I wandered past the address, deciphering what I could from the small row house. All the curtains were pulled shut. The house was certainly not the house of a wealthy family, nor was it the house of a poor family. In short, I could tell nothing about the house.

"I kept walking, not wanting to arouse any suspicion. For the rest of the morning, I looped through the neighborhood, always scanning the faces for Agata. Every now and then I returned to the street, sometimes to walk past the house and sometimes only to look down the bending road. Finally, midway through the morning, I was strolling toward the house when I saw two women. They were approaching from the opposite direction. I slowed down and watched surreptitiously. The two women, who seemed to be near to my age, were dressed in very drab black clothing, almost rags. Their heads were covered in the same drab black cloth. When I saw them go into the house, my heart dropped. I thought certainly they were in mourning clothes.

"As I watched them enter, I caught sight of movement at one of the windows. A woman in black was looking out at me. She quickly let the curtain fall in front of her. I continued past, still not wanting to go to the door, and afraid that I had drawn their attention. I became more careful after that. I only watched from afar. Throughout the day, I saw more of the same. Women of all ages, dressed in black clothing, coming and going from the house, always in groups of at least two. I could only assume one thing."

"Shiva."

"Of course. What else could it be? Someone had died in the house. But still, not everything made sense. Why did only women attend? That day was Friday. I went back to my hosts in the late afternoon to prepare for Shabbat. Later that evening, I told them I had noticed mourners in the neighborhood. I wondered if they knew who had died. They shook their heads. I did not press it. I was feeling uncomfortable, as though I was doing wrong. I did not want to lose the trust of my hosts.

"The next day, I went out again into the neighborhood, again hoping that maybe I would see Agata's face. I wandered around again, always casually circling past the street. I saw no one, until the middle of the afternoon. I saw a large group of women, all dressed in black, the same as the day before. As I expected, they all went into the house. Ah ha! I thought."

"You don't sit shiva on Shabbat."

"Exactly," said Grandpa Moshe. "But I still did not understand anything about the house. When I went back to my hosts that afternoon, I could no longer resist asking them. I explained that I had come in search of my lost wife. I showed them the street address. They looked long at each other before speaking.

"The man said to me, 'My friend, do not go to that house. You can only find sadness. Your wife is no longer there.'

"The house, he told me, was closed off to the world. Do you think that would stop me?"

Aaron shook his head.

"Of course not. The next day, I went to the door and knocked. I had to knock and knock until someone would answer. Finally, an older woman dressed in black opened the door. I told her I was looking for Agata. She told me that no woman named Agata was there. She attempted to close the door, but I stopped the door with my hand. I told her I was her husband. She repeated that no woman named Agata was there.

"I stepped away, and the woman pressed the door closed as she watched me. I stood in the road, staring up at the house. Hours passed. No one came or went. I knocked again at the door, and the same older woman appeared, a few strands of gray hair visible beneath a black head covering. Before I could speak, she told me that no woman named Agata was there. I told her I would be standing outside. She nodded understandingly and shut the door.

"I was given hope by her sympathetic expression, but no one came from the house. For hours, I sat on the stoop. For hours, I considered why she had nodded with such understanding. And so I was not surprised when she came outside to me as the light of the summer day began to fade. I stood up. She looked into my eyes. She urged me to leave and never come back. She told me what I had already realized: I was not the first husband to knock on that door.

"I thanked her and left, and perhaps she thought that she would not see me again. I myself wasn't certain what I would do next. What was clear to me was that this was a house of women who had given up all the things of this world. To see Agata would be to see a ghost. I could only cause myself pain; I could only cause her pain. I weighed the moral reasons to stay and to go. In the end, I was still too young—too headstrong. When the sun was down, I went back to the house where I was staying. But I returned the next morning after breakfast. I did not knock on the door. I sat against a wall across the road with a book in my hands, as I had done during so much of my youth.

"The day after that, I did the same. As long as the sun was in the sky, I waited outside the house. I saw many women come and go, but never Agata. I assumed she was inside, avoiding me. But I also wondered if I had been mistaken, especially as my hope dwindled. Maybe my patron in New York only knew of this house where so many women had ended up, and didn't know for certain that Agata was there. Maybe he had thought that another woman was my wife. My patron hadn't told me anything! I knew nothing! Those were the doubts going through my head as I slowly sank into despair, sitting against the wall with my book.

"Finally, on the third day, I was ready to give up hope. When the sun dipped below the horizon, I went to the door and knocked. No one came, as I expected. I knocked again, and the same older woman came, as I expected. As soon as the door cracked open, I began to speak. But the woman bowed her head and held up her hand to silence me. She backed away and opened the door for me to enter. I stepped into the house, and the door closed behind me. The woman gestured toward a doorway and nodded.

"I was trembling. I thought I might faint. I wandered into a small, dim room where two chairs had been placed on opposite sides. I looked around in wonder. All the walls of the small room were lined with beautiful old books from floor to ceiling. Books were arranged row upon row in wooden shelves built into the walls. Only I was too distracted by thoughts of Agata to look any more closely.

"The older woman gestured toward one of the chairs. Once I was seated, she disappeared. I waited in fear. I was in a daze. I could not believe what was happening. And suddenly she appeared. Dressed in a black shroud, her head covered in black cloth, her face concealed behind a black veil, she drifted across the room. I could do nothing but stare. I was frozen. She sat down in the chair on the opposite side of the room.

" 'Agata,' I whispered.

"She did not respond. She gazed at the bare wood floor. I said her name again, and she lifted her eyes. Seeing into her face, I was completely overcome. I began to sob—tears of sadness, tears of joy.

" 'Agata,' I pleaded.

"Still, she said nothing. And she dropped her eyes again. I continued to wipe away tears, until I could no longer resist. I stood up, but she stopped me. She raised her hand. Once more, she raised her eyes to me.

" 'I am not Agata,' she said. 'I am Tabitha.'

"Her words pierced me. Her voice sent shivers through me—a voice I had known nearly my whole life, from when we were children. Her voice was the same, and yet different. She was transformed. She spoke not just as a woman who had been through hell—a woman who had known life and who had known death—but as a woman of great authority. When she spoke, I immediately was intimidated. I shrank. I was small. I felt exposed. Before she said anything else, I was ashamed that I had left Poland, that I had moved on. All of us who had suffered in the camps had been to an unearthly place, but I knew then that she had chosen to remain there.

"The sun had now fallen, and the room had gone dark. I waited, stupefied, as she lit a gas lamp. When she sat back down, she spoke.

" 'Moshe,' she said, 'you must go back to your home. You do not live here anymore. Your place is not here. Your place is not with me.'

"Her words brought more tears to my eyes. I could not say a word.

" 'My life is not my own,' she said.

"She stood up to go, and I could see for the first time that she too was deeply pained by this. She refused to show any emotion, but I knew that she was suffering. I wanted to fall at her feet and beg her not to leave. She went to the doorway and stopped.

" 'Return here tomorrow at sunset,' she said.

"With that, she left the room. By then, I was sitting in the dim light of the sole gas lamp. The older woman returned shortly and showed me to the door."

Grandpa Moshe's voice drifted off. He was lost in thought. Aaron shuffled up in bed, hoping to wake him from his trance. The sun had now begun to rise. The fading moon was nearly out of sight. Grandpa Moshe's eyes, laden with tears, gleamed in the light of dawn. He stood up from his chair.

"Are you okay, grandpa?"

"Yes, Aaron. That is enough for now. I must sleep."

Chapter Eight

A Quiet Saturday

Aaron slept late. When he woke, he went straight to Grandpa Moshe's room at the end of the hallway. His grandfather was still in bed, a motionless heap beneath the blankets. Downstairs, he found a note on the dining room table from his mother. She was at the university all day for a symposium.

Aaron ate breakfast. He did the dishes. He waited for Grandpa Moshe to wake up.

He heard nothing from the floor above, not even the creaky bed. Around noon, he went back upstairs to check on his grandfather. Evidently, he was still fast asleep, and Aaron had learned from a young age not to disturb him. He wondered if Grandpa Moshe was not only exhausted from being up all night, but emotionally depleted from recounting the story of Agata. Aaron was desperate to know the next part of the saga.

After lunch, Aaron laid out his college homework at the dining room table, his ears attuned to the floor above. Finally, in the middle of the afternoon, he heard Grandpa Moshe's bed creak. He heard footsteps on the floorboards. Aaron listened intently from the kitchen table. At last, he could no longer resist. He slipped up the stairs and knocked at the door. He could hear Grandpa Moshe moving around. He knocked again.

"Don't come in," grumbled Grandpa Moshe.

Aaron waited outside the door, unsure what to say. Grandpa Moshe had stopped moving around the room.

"Grandpa Moshe?" said Aaron. "Are you okay?"

"Yes. I must rest."

"Do you need anything?"

"I must rest."

His voice betrayed more than a hint of annoyance. Crestfallen, Aaron returned to the dining room table, back to his homework, but quickly shut his books. In the late afternoon, as the day was darkening, his mother returned from the university. She put out the leftovers in Styrofoam from the night before. They ate together in near silence.

"Has your grandfather been down?" she asked.

Aaron shook his head.

"Have you checked on him?"

"He got up, but he didn't want to be disturbed."

Aaron's mother nodded. When they had finished eating, she stood up with her dishes and went to the kitchen. She appeared again in the doorway with her sleeves rolled up.

"You know, sweetie," she said. "Grandpa Moshe is a little bit of a storyteller."

Aaron glared at her. She shrugged and raised her eyebrows as she went back into the kitchen. Aaron followed her with his dishes and put them in the sink.

"Why do you say that?" he asked.

"I noticed he was in your room last night," she said.

"What did you hear?"

"I didn't hear anything."

Aaron watched her. She rinsed off the dishes and dried off her hands and began putting together a plate of food for Grandpa Moshe.

"Mom," said Aaron, "Did you ever find out what happened to my dad?"

"Nope."

"Nothing at all?"

"Nothing at all."

"Do you know where he is?"

She huffed and clattered the plate of food onto the kitchen counter.

"Why are you asking me this all the sudden? What did Grandpa Moshe say?"

"Nothing, mom. He didn't say anything about that. I was just curious."

"He's dead, okay? You're old enough to know."

"Okay."

"I'm going to bring your grandfather some food."

"Okay."

"Remember what I said about Grandpa Moshe."

"Okay."

Chapter Nine

A Shocking Discovery

The next morning, Aaron again went straight to Grandpa Moshe's room, and again he was still in bed. Throughout the day, Aaron went up to check on him, but the door remained closed. Aaron's mother brought him his meals. She told Aaron it was best not to bother him. He was not doing well, and Aaron would only get him worked up. Aaron delayed his departure, hoping his grandfather would emerge from his room, but he never appeared. In the early evening, Aaron decided he could no longer put off his drive back to school. The whole way, he was plagued by curiosity and doubt.

On Monday morning, he went to the library and got himself situated at a carrel. As he pulled books out of his backpack, he caught sight of the large envelope with the picture, which had somehow slipped his mind. Aaron slid the envelope out from between two books and set it down on his desk. He stood up in shock. Taped to the front of the envelope was a scrap of paper with a handwritten note in shaky block letters:

"HIS NAME IS LAZARUS."

Aaron's mind raced. He could not understand what he was seeing. All at once he remembered the part of Professor Freeman's story he had somehow forgotten. He had not said anything to Grandpa Moshe about any Lazarus. When had his grandfather written the note? He must have snuck downstairs in the night!

Aaron stood up from his desk and grabbed the envelope. Leaving his things behind, he darted out of the library and across the frozen quad, the envelope swinging in his hand. He barged into the humanities building and ran down the hallway. Out of breath, he knocked on the door to Professor Freeman's office. He heard nothing but saw a crack of light beneath the door. He knocked again more forcefully.

"One moment, please," the professor sing-song-ed irritably.

Aaron waited impatiently, trying to catch his breath. He could hear shuffling inside. At last, the door swung open.

"Yes?" said Professor Freeman.

Aaron pushed past the professor into the spacious office walled with bookshelves. He stood in the middle of the room with the envelope in his hand. The professor came around his desk. He stood over it, propping himself up on his arms.

"What is it?" said the professor.

"Why did you have me read that Bible story?" said Aaron.

"Are you okay?"

"I'm fine," said Aaron. "I just want to know why you had me read it."

"Well, there's more to the story, Aaron. You left before I could finish." Professor Freeman paused. "Are you sure you're okay?"

"Yes. What is the rest of the story?"

"Aaron, I have to tell you, I appreciate your enthusiasm, but could we perhaps do this another time? I am in the middle of something."

"Why did you have me read it?" demanded Aaron.

"Ah, I see you've brought me my envelope back," said the professor. "Good."

"Why?" said Aaron. "I need to know!"

Professor Freeman stopped. He grew sober. He bowed his head and walked back around. He propped himself up against the desk and crossed his arms.

"Can you please tell me?"

"Okay, okay. Just relax."

"I'm fine."

"That day at Princeton," he said, "there was something else the man told us."

"What did he say?"

Professor Freeman sighed. He put his head in his hand.

"That day at Princeton, there was something else the man told us. He gave us a name."

"What name?"

"The name of the man, or the name the man gave us—you've probably guessed by now—was Lazarus."

Aaron swallowed and nodded, turning pale.

"He called himself Lazarus."

"As in the Lazarus of John Chapter 11."

"That's right. As in the brother of Mary and Martha; as in the man from Bethany whom Jesus raised from the dead."

Aaron shook his head, still holding the envelope in his hand.

"You see, as he described to us," said the professor, "once you've been called forth from the tomb, you can't very well go back to being dead."

Professor Freeman began to chuckle, but Aaron interrupted him.

"So then he roamed the earth," said Aaron.

"Well, yes. In theory. Essentially, he had already been resurrected, before all the rest of us, so he was waiting for Judgment Day. Until that day, he wandered the earth, suffering with his people—he told us all this."

Aaron set down the envelope in front of Professor Freeman.

"Look at this."

"What do you mean?"

Aaron stared Professor Freeman in the eyes. He tapped the note with his finger. The professor turned ashen.

"My God," said Professor Freeman. "Your grandfather knew him."

Chapter Ten

Reconnaissance Mission

Professor Freeman sat back in his desk chair and listened in disbelief. Aaron explained how his grandfather had reacted upon seeing the picture, how he had behaved as though he had never seen the person. He summarized Grandpa Moshe's years after the war, leaving out the story about his trip to Poland to find Agata.

"You didn't find out more?" the professor exclaimed. "What sort of historian are you?"

"I couldn't!" said Aaron. "He was in bed."

"Oh, sure, he was. Sneaking around in the middle of the night leaving clues behind—that sounds like a sick old man to me, all right. Anyway, we must go speak with him."

"I'll see what I can do."

Aaron called his mother that night. He asked her how Grandpa Moshe was doing. She said he was still worn down. She wouldn't let him talk on the phone. Aaron tried to express how important it was, but she wouldn't budge.

"Are you trying to kill him?"

"Mom, I just want to talk to him."

"He's exhausted! He can't talk. The poor man has suffered enough."

Aaron called back the next day, and the day after that, and still his mother wouldn't put Grandpa Moshe on the phone.

"What do you want to talk to him about, anyway?" she asked.

"Nothing. I just want to talk to him."

"You want to talk to him about one of his stories, don't you. I told you, Aaron, you can't believe everything Grandpa Moshe tells you."

And every day, Professor Freeman demanded to know if he had found out anything else, until finally he lost patience. After class that week, Professor Freeman pulled Aaron aside.

"That's it," he said. "I've had enough. We're going."

That Friday around noon, Professor Freeman picked Aaron up at the loop outside his dorm, handing him a coffee as he got in the car.

"Isn't this exciting?"

"I guess so," said Aaron.

"Come on! Where's your sense of adventure!"

Aaron took a deep breath and sipped from his coffee cup.

"Now," said the professor, "have I ever told you about my mentor at Dartmouth?"

The whole drive, Professor Freeman regaled him with tale after tale of his encounters with prominent writers and public figures. He was a brilliant raconteur, but all his stories were about the same humble professor who somehow managed to brush shoulders with the high and mighty. Aaron had never been more relieved to see his front door.

They rang the doorbell. No one came. Aaron unlocked the door with his spare key. The house was dim. No lights were on.

"Wait here," said Aaron.

Professor Freeman wandered into the dining room and sat down at the table. Aaron checked the living room. He went upstairs and saw that Grandpa Moshe's door was still closed. He knocked gently. He inched the door open and poked his head inside. The bed was made. No one was there. Aaron sauntered down the stairs slowly, wondering what they should do next. He assumed Grandpa Moshe was up and about again and had gone to campus to read the newspaper in his office.

As Aaron came around the corner into the dining room, he saw Grandpa Moshe sneaking out of the kitchen with a paring knife in one hand and a copper-bottom pot in the other. The unsuspecting Professor Freeman was staring at his phone with his back to the kitchen.

"Grandpa, no!" yelled Aaron.

But Grandpa Moshe was already bringing down the pot onto Professor Freeman's head with a resounding metallic boing. Professor Freeman crumpled. He fell off his chair as if knocked out cold. Grandpa Moshe stood over him in confusion, the pot and the paring knife raised and ready. Aaron ran over to look. Professor Freeman appeared to be unconscious. But after a suspenseful moment, he let out a long howl. He curled up in a fetal position and rubbed his head vigorously.

"That's my professor!"

"How was I to know?" said Grandpa Moshe. "What are you doing here?"

"I told mom I was coming."

"You know she doesn't tell me anything!"

"Where were you? I was looking all over the house."

"I was in the bathroom! Can't a man go to the bathroom?"

Professor Freeman had sat up. He stopped rubbing his head. He was staring, his jaw slack. Grandpa Moshe looked down at him in stunned silence.

"Michael?"

"Professor?"

"What?" said Aaron.

"You're Aaron's professor?"

"You're Aaron's grandfather?"

"You old clown! I can't believe it!" said Grandpa Moshe.

"What were you going to do with that knife?" said Professor Freeman. "Peel me?"

They both broke down in laughter.

"What is going on?" said Aaron.

"Amazing," said Grandpa Moshe. "Your professor here was my student!"

Aaron tried to make sense of it all as Grandpa Moshe gave Professor Freeman a hand. They examined each other.

"You look the same," said Professor Freeman.

"You, too," said Grandpa Moshe, "except for a few hairs on your head."

"I kept as many as I could."

"Sit! Sit!"

Aaron fixed the two men a cup of tea as they chatted in the living room, catching up on the last decades, and inquiring after old acquaintances.

"You know, Aaron, I knew your professor when he was just a freshman psychology student. But even back then you would have thought he knew everything."

"I've always been myself," admitted Professor Freeman. "No one can deny that."

"But I don't understand," said Aaron. "You taught at Dartmouth?"

"Dartmouth? What? No. I was at Rutgers my whole career."

Professor Freeman turned a deep red and bowed his head low over his cup of tea as he took a sip.

"What did you tell him?" said Grandpa Moshe.

"Well, you see—you remember, don't you—I did that summer program at Dartmouth."

"What? That summer language camp thing?"

"Well, yes. It was more than that."

Grandpa Moshe put down his cup of tea with a guffaw and slapped his knee. Professor Freeman smiled coyly.

"I never exactly told anyone I graduated from Dartmouth."

"I love it," said Grandpa Moshe. "You're the same old conman."

"Guilty as charged."

Grandpa Moshe cuffed his old student, who nearly spilled his tea on himself. Aaron looked on with a smirk.

"But anyway, what are you two doing here?" said Grandpa Moshe. "Did you drive all the way here to surprise me?"

"No," said Aaron. "We had no idea."

"Yeah? What is it?"

Aaron and Professor Freeman exchanged a glance.

"Well," said Professor Freeman. "I saw the note you left for Aaron. I was intrigued."

"What?"

"The note," said Aaron. "The note you put on the picture."

"What are you talking about?"

"When I got back to school, I found a note on the envelope."

Aaron went to his backpack at the front door. He handed his grandfather the large envelope, the note still attached.

"Oh, no. This note? Please don't tell me you drove all the way back here just to ask me about this."

"We had to know," said Professor Freeman.

Grandpa Moshe set the envelope down on the table. He said nothing for a moment, only shaking his head. Professor Freeman and Aaron watched him. When he spoke, his voice trembled with suppressed anger.

"Michael, are you serious?"

"What do you mean?"

"I cannot believe that you are perpetuating this nonsense!"

Professor Freeman leaned back, his eyes widening.

"You're a real fool, you know that? And you're hurting these students. And my grandson is one of them! How many people have you told this crap to?"

"What do you mean? I've barely told a soul what I told Aaron!"

"Of course you haven't. You have to size up your dupe first."

"That is simply not true!"

Grandpa Moshe stood up. He shook his head bitterly and walked to the window.

"I'm sorry, Aaron," he said, "but you've been had. Your professor here has always been a conman. I thought he would have grown up by now."

"This is preposterous! You can say anything you like, but I did not tell your grandson a single lie. I told him exactly the truth as I know it."

"Well, then, you're the dupe."

"But I don't understand," said Aaron. "How did you know that it was Lazarus?"

Grandpa Moshe bowed his head and clasped his hands behind his back.

"Of course, I knew it was Lazarus. I'm sorry to say, Aaron, you've been roped into a very, very old joke. These fantastic stories have been circulating forever. And it's fools like your professor here that keep them alive."

"Why didn't you just tell me that?"

"I told you it was nonsense, and that's exactly what it is. I didn't want to make you think it was anything more than a silly tall tale made up by a bunch of academics with too much time on their hands. The last thing we need in this world is another rumor about some nefarious Jewish conspiracy."

"Aaron," said Professor Freeman. "I promise I never said a false word to you."

"But grandpa, why did you leave the note?" said Aaron.

"I'm sorry, Aaron. It was a dumb joke. I shouldn't have done it. I had no idea you took this thing so seriously."

"Then it was a cruel joke," said Professor Freeman.

He stood up and left the room.

"I'm sorry, Aaron," said Grandpa Moshe. "Michael is right. It was a cruel joke. I didn't mean it to be."

Aaron dropped his head. Grandpa Moshe put his hand on Aaron's shoulder.

"I'm sorry."

Professor Freeman was already at the front door.

"Are you ready to go?" he called. "We're going."

"Yeah," said Aaron. "I guess we should go."

Chapter Eleven

An Unexpected Visit

Professor Freeman prattled on as he drove, defending himself against Grandpa Moshe's accusations as if he was sitting in the back seat. Aaron gazed at the passing scenery, tuning him out. He felt betrayed by everyone—betrayed by Professor Freeman for telling him the fairy tale, betrayed by his grandfather for pulling a prank on him, instead of just telling him the truth. But more than anything, he felt embarrassed. He had been an idiot. Professor Freeman might have been a fool, but Aaron was the bigger fool for listening to him.

Night was falling as they turned onto the main campus road. Professor Freeman, reduced to frustrated mutterings, dropped Aaron off near his dorm room without more than a goodbye. Aaron went to his room and fell onto his bed in a stupor. He had been living a sort of twisted dream. He wished he could somehow scrub his mind clear of all the nonsense. Regretting his stupidity, he dozed off in the early evening.

He awoke with a start to the noise of passing students in the hallway. The sky was dark. Small lamps illuminated the campus paths outside his window. He put his head back down on his pillow, staring up at the ceiling. Hearing a soft knock, he craned his neck up. He could see a shadow in the strip of bright light beneath his door. He heard another soft knock. Aaron groggily got out of bed. He flicked on his light and opened the door. He almost thought he was hallucinating.

"Grandpa?"

"Hi, Aaron."

"What are you doing here?"

"I drove straight here," said Grandpa Moshe. "I'm sorry. I had no choice. The things I have to say I could not say in front of Michael. He was one of my best students, but he can be a first-class clown. Intelligence and sense are two different things."

Aaron opened the door, squinting sleepily. He picked his dirty clothes up off the floor and threw them into the laundry bin and pulled out his desk chair. Grandpa Moshe sat down.

"There's much more to this story. Do you remember what I said when I saw the picture?"

Aaron shrugged, still bleary-eyed, and shook his head.

"I said it was my old philosophy professor."

"Right," Aaron said, sighing a laugh. "I remember."

"Aaron," said Grandpa Moshe, "I wasn't lying."

"What?"

"Lock the door."

Chapter Twelve

The Lazarus of Lodz

"I'll pick up where I left off," began Grandpa Moshe. "If you remember, I was in Lodz. My beloved Agata had broken my heart. But she had given me a lifeline. She told me to come back the next day at sunset.

"Of course, her words had been clear. I knew, rationally, that Agata was no longer Agata. She was a new person. She was not my wife. She was not even the person I had known. But how could I give up hope? My brain told me to be reasonable. My heart would not listen. The next day, I sat across the street from her door the entire afternoon, waiting for the sun to fall.

"As soon as the sun touched the horizon, I noticed the door move. I got to my feet and watched. The older woman, who had let me in the day before, appeared in the doorway. She stood aside as another woman, dressed all in black, with a black head covering, came out. Yet another woman, dressed the same way, followed her, and another and another. A whole troupe of these women filed out, assembling in pairs outside the house, in two loose lines like an elementary school class going out for a field trip. One of the last to come out was my dear Agata. My heart ached to see her. She did not look at me.

"When they had all come out of the house, the older woman locked the door behind them. She went to the front of the group, and she looked at me—a knowing look. She led the two lines of women down the street. What a macabre group it was! You would have thought it was a funeral procession. Toward the end of the line was Agata. As they began to move, she stole a glance at me, and I understood I was to follow.

"I stayed back, not wanting to cause any trouble for Agata. And I was also a little afraid to be associated with this strange group. As we went along, I noticed people stared from their houses. Some shut their doors or clattered their shutters closed, as if to ward off evil spirits. When we got into the busier section of the neighborhood, people made way for the women in black. They cleared the sidewalks. Some people bowed their heads. One old man even got down onto his knees. It was a holy group—full of strange spiritual energy. You can't explain it. We don't have that sort of thing in America. Anyone could feel their presence as they went by.

"The sky darkened as we passed through the town, meandering through the old streets. Suddenly, I found that we were far from the crowded center of the neighborhood. The line turned down a narrow cobblestone street, almost an alleyway, not large enough for a car. As soon as the last woman had gone, I ran after them and poked my head around the corner. The women in black had stopped, and the older woman was counting her group. When she finished, she returned to the front of the line, and one at a time the women began disappearing like little black rabbits, ducking into an entryway below street level.

"Again, I waited for them all to go before chasing after them. Midway down the narrow cobblestone street, I came to a small, dark staircase, which almost seemed to be carved into the ground. For the first time, I was afraid. The staircase was unmarked. No one was in sight now, and the last light of day was fading. My imagination was running wild. I had the feeling I was entering some sort of ancient torture chamber. How could I know I wasn't being trapped? I still knew nothing about this bizarre cult. But I had come so far, and my sweet Agata was inside. Turning back was not an option. I threw caution to the wind and hurried down the staircase.

"At the bottom of the stairs, I found a heavy door with iron hinges, a medieval doorway too low to enter without bending. In the very last shred of daylight, I felt around for a doorknob, but I found nothing. I smoothed my hands up and down the old wood and ran my fingers along the cracks. I pulled at the edges with the tips of my fingers. The door was closed from the other side. I stepped back and sat down on the stone stairs behind me. I was stuck.

"But then the door opened a crack. I jumped to my feet and grabbed the door before it could close again. I slowly inched the door open and crouched slightly to go through the doorway. On the other side was Agata. Our eyes met, and I was full of relief.

" 'Thank you,' I whispered.

"She merely nodded. She turned, and darted ahead, and almost immediately she was out of sight. I was in a tunnel, lit only by electric lamps, like you see in an old coal mine. My eyes adjusted, and I realized I was in a passageway with stone walls and a stone ceiling. These tunnels were a part of a massive underground network dating back hundreds of years. Jews and resistance fighters had used this tunnel system throughout the war. I didn't know that at the time. I only knew to keep walking, following the direction of Agata.

"I walked for several minutes through the darkness, always following the next dim electric light, every step leading me deeper into the bowels of this subterranean world. The tunnel twisted and turned, and I saw other passageways. I pressed forward doubtfully, not knowing if I was going in the right direction, straining my eyes in the darkness, praying I would see Agata. At last, as I came around a bend, I caught sight of a flitting figure, a shadow. I stopped instinctively, jolted. Agata raised her head, and her eyes gleamed. Our eyes again met for a fleeting moment, and she was off again down the passageway.

"I could see now that she was leading me toward the end, toward a light in the distance that bent around the stone walls of the tunnel. And finally, I saw a lit entryway—a wall of pale light—and Agata's silhouette. She passed through into the pale light and was gone. I slowed as I came closer to the opening, not knowing what was beyond. I crept along and peeked my head into the next room. A shiver ran through me. I will never forget the sight.

"I had come to a large arched room, in the belly of the city, full of dark figures. The underground hall was lit by the same electric lights that ran along the walls of the tunnel. A group of fifty people was seated on austere wooden chairs, facing away from me, toward a blank stone wall. The arrangement was eerie, and at first I was terrified. I could not understand why they were assembled that way. But I soon saw that in the front of the room was a sort of dais. They were waiting for someone.

"I sat down quietly in the last row of chairs. No one spoke to each other. Everyone stared at the stone wall. I searched out Agata among the group of women in black, but I could only guess which one she was. They all sat perfectly still, facing forward. Finally, an arched door held together with black iron, similar to the one I had used to enter the tunnel, slowly drifted open. The room was already silent, but somehow the open door created an added hush. We were all holding our breath! The atmosphere became even more holy. A sacred stillness swept over the room. I could feel my heart beating in my chest. Then a small man, all alone, entered through the door. And his presence was overwhelming. I sensed I was seeing someone superhuman. At the risk of blasphemy, I would say I was seeing a sort of god."

"Lazarus," whispered Aaron.

"Lazarus," said Grandpa Moshe. "The Lazarus of Lodz. He was just as you have seen in the picture, dressed in a hooded black shroud, with a long gray beard. He was a ghost. His eyes shined with pure light. As

I said, I was at the back of the hall, and still his clear eyes were piercing. He inhabited a different realm. Time stopped when he entered the room. My whole attention was absorbed by this figure, even before he began to talk. But when he began to talk! Aaron, I cannot describe to you the effect he had. The whole room was enthralled from the moment he opened his mouth until he abruptly stood up and left. Only then did I realize I had been under a spell."

"What did he say?" asked Aaron.

"Oh, he said so much—I cannot tell you. He told the sorts of stories you must have heard already, maybe even the same stories. He was an encyclopedia. He was more than that. He was a phenomenon. He knew everything. He knew it because he had lived it. And when he spoke, doubt could not enter your mind. Only later could you think that this man had to be a magician, or a lunatic genius."

"But what did he tell you?"

"If I could tell you all that he told us, I too would be a genius. I can no longer remember all the history he related in those few hours."

Grandpa Moshe hesitated and sat back in his chair. He smiled distantly as he threw his chin up and shook his head.

"What?" said Aaron.

"One story did stay with me. I have never been able to get it out of my head. You will understand why."

"What was it?"

"First, you must remember, Aaron, there were stories great and small. He told us of concentration camps and of pogroms, and those are the tales that always survive behind the closed doors of dark corridors. But there was more to what he said. The last story he told us was a story full of sadness, full of hope. It was also a story of horror, and that is where it begins, in a small town in what was then Flanders."

Chapter Thirteen

Lysbette van Slecht

"I will tell you of a woman whose evil has never been surpassed. I cannot say how she became the wicked woman that she was. I can only tell you that I have never heard of any person capable of more cruelty than she. Her name was Lysbette van Slecht.

"Lysbette van Slecht is not an important figure in history—not in any way. Her name is recorded in the various registries from the fifteenth century, for she was a woman of minor prominence in her town. She was part of the landed gentry.

"In that region, at that time, the Jews were limited in what they could do for a living. All across Europe, they could hold only certain occupations. In this town, the Jews were restricted from the various trades, and so were forced to farm. But, of course, they were not permitted to own land. They were given parcels of land, as serfs. Even then, they were unwelcome. Other lowly farmers did not want their competition. If the peasants had had the power of the tradesmen in the town, they would have banned the Jews even from working the land. And the landowners themselves did not want them around, with one exception: Lysbette van Slecht.

"Lysbette was known in the community as a strange woman. She did not participate in any of the town activities. She hadn't always kept to herself, however. In her youth, she had been a great beauty, and she was sophisticated. She may not have been the highest nobility, but she was elegant and educated. She punched above her weight, and she succeeded in knocking out a marquis, the son of the Baron van Hofstede. They began their married life on his family's estate, which soon, as events unfolded, became her estate. For not more than three years into their marriage, the marquis was dead.

"The family had no evidence, but they were suspicious. The illness had come and gone in a flash. The sickness, they could see, was real. His corpse was riddled with all the marks of plague. Still, the family could not understand how a healthy man could fall victim to a plague that was nowhere else in the region. They did not trust this woman, who showed no sadness, whose soul seemed blacker and blacker every time they saw her. Yet they found they were frightened of her. She had a power over them. And that was how she stayed on the estate that she otherwise should not have inherited according to the laws.

"This estate was separate from the town, a large tract of land far off from any other properties. And as I said, she was the only landowner who accepted Jews as workers, and so Jewish laborers, new to the area, sought her out. Jews came from far off in search of work. As the years passed, she also became known for accepting other people who could not find work elsewhere. She accepted certain criminals, exiled from their towns, drunks who had been banned from returning home, and various other unwanted people.

"At first, the people of the town, who could know very little of what went on in the estate, assumed the obvious. That is, they assumed the best. Maybe you can guess."

Grandpa Moshe paused, prompting Aaron.

"That she was taking these people in?"

"Yes, of course. What else could you think? She was a sort of saint. She was running a charity. In any case, she had lost her husband. She had to manage the property all on her own. They had other workers, no doubt, but workers were in demand."

"But that wasn't the case."

"No, no, no, no, no. That was not the case. Lysbette never left the estate, and that was normal. The people of the town had grown used to that. What was strange was that no one else ever came from the estate. Within months after the marquis's death, the produce from the land dried up entirely. Previously, they had sold the excess produce to the tradesmen in the town. Suddenly that stopped. No laborers came to the town; no produce came to the town. The estate had become an island.

"Again, at first, this was not strange. They assumed she was struggling to oversee the estate. Many people in the town talked. They said, this was why a woman could not inherit property. And no one wanted to go see. No one dared go near the property. By then, rumors about her husband's death had spread, and word that she was a witch became the stuff of legend.

"Now stop to remember, however, that not everyone had the luxury of avoiding her estate. Desperate workers, outcasts, without any other chance of survival, chose to go to her for work rather than starve. What befell them was much worse.

"I can see," said Grandpa Moshe, "that you are putting it together in your head: Jews in need of work, petty criminals, drunks, outcasts of every description—they all went to her in desperation. Do you understand what I'm telling you, Aaron?"

Aaron nodded.

"Yes, Aaron. She was committing her own holocaust."

"How did they find out?"

"I am getting there, slowly. Despite all their suspicions, the people of the town were not in any rush to find out what was going on. They merely told their children to stay far away. As long as the evil was not at their doorstep, they were happy not to get involved. So it has always been, so it will always be.

"Yet one day in the late summer, as the harvest season approached, a man knocked at the great doors of the mansion. This was unusual, for a mere serf knew better than to approach the grand entrance. Lysbette's head servant answered the door. These workers were under her spell. The men who had been part of the estate under her husband had become slaves to her evil will. They had cooperated with her all along, at first not knowing what else to do. Over time, they had grown to believe in her cause, blinding themselves to the depravity of their acts.

"The head servant, the man who had overseen the property under the marquis, had become the chief executor of Lysbette's schemes. When he opened the door, at first he saw an old man, the type of old man who so often would show up at the door that time of year—probably a drunk, anxious to work one last harvest season in hopes of surviving the winter. Only this was no ordinary old man. The head servant immediately detected that this was not like the other desperate people who came to the door.

"All the same, with an unctuous smile, he told the old man to go around to the laborers' quarters, for indeed they needed the labor, they needed the help. The old man did not smile. He did not nod. He only looked at the head servant, and the head servant trembled beneath his hard outer layer.

" 'I am here to see Lysbette,' said the old man.

"The head servant scoffed. Even though he sensed this was no ordinary man, he was set in his ways. His heart had been hardened. Again, he told the old man to go to the workers' quarters. The old man did not move.

" 'I am here to see Lysbette,' he said again.

"Now the head servant's rage quickly leapt up like a flame doused in kerosene. He had a mind to murder the old man where he stood, to beat him to death for his insolence. He grabbed the man by his cloak and told him to get out of his sight if he wanted to live. The old man did not flinch.

" 'I am here to see Lysbette,' he said.

"Suddenly, near to the old man, seeing into his eyes, the head servant was terrified. He sensed the judgment of God himself. Rattled, he released the old man and stood back.

" 'What do you want?' he said.

" 'I am here to see Lysbette,' said the old man.

"The head servant stepped into the house, spellbound, and opened the door wide for the man to come through. The massive estate house had become dusty and dark, full of the spirit of the people who lived there. All the heavy curtains were pulled shut. Only slivers of sunlight passed into the house. The head servant motioned for the old man to wait in the sitting room. He left him there to go find Lysbette.

"He knocked at her door gently, as he always did. He was sweating with fear, not knowing how to tell her what had happened. The door slowly opened.

" 'There is an old man here,' he began.

" 'I know. I have seen from my window. Serve the man stew,' she said. 'I will come down when I am ready.'

"The head servant went back downstairs and was horrified to find that the curtains were open. The sun was pouring into the sitting room, and the old man was sitting in the stream of light. The head servant immediately went to the curtains to pull them shut.

" 'Do not do that,' said the old man. 'I have come to bring light.'

"As if physically controlled by the words, the head servant stopped where he was. Unable to bear the presence of the old man, he hurried out of the room, and out to the laborers' quarters, where stew was kept for the workers. As he had been instructed many times before, he prepared a bowl of poisoned stew. He brought the bowl into the house and set it down at the banqueting table with a cup of water and a crust of bread. He summoned the old man.

"Without a word, or any apparent suspicion, the old man sat down to the bowl. The head servant watched intently as the old man quietly ate the stew. When he had finished, he set down his utensil and stared at the head servant, causing the head servant to fidget. Normally, the poison took effect immediately. The old man was unfazed. He kept his eyes fixed on the head servant until the head servant could no longer bear his gaze. He left the room.

"Before long, Lysbette van Slecht's footsteps sounded on the floor above. She came down the stairs slowly, her every step reverberating through the cavernous mansion. The old man waited for her where he sat. He did not stand when she entered the room. She sat down at the other end of the table. Their eyes met, and they dueled in absolute silence. Lysbette's eyes were black with the soot of her sin, and when she spoke, her voice was not her own.

" 'You have eaten the stew,' she said, 'and yet you sit.'

"The old man said nothing. Lysbette's lips curled into a smile.

" 'I know you,' she said. 'I have met the one who sent you.'

"Again, the old man did not speak. He nodded once.

" 'You have no power over me,' she said.

"Every time Lysbette opened her mouth, she sneered and became more agitated. The wrath inside of her boiled up. The old man spoke.

" 'I have come to free you.'

" 'You cannot free me!' she shrieked.

"Lysbette stood up from the table, knocking down her chair. She gnashed her teeth and pulled at her hair. The old man did not move. His penetrating eyes rested on Lysbette, and his gaze seemed to burn her.

" 'Get out!' she screamed.

"The old man's stillness drove her into the throes of insanity. She dashed to the sideboard for a carving knife and rushed across the room at the old man, who did not move. Coming upon him, she raised the carving knife above her head with both hands and let out a horrifying cry."

Grandpa Moshe paused, his eyes wide, his hands above his head. He gradually lowered his arms as he continued quietly.

"But she was stopped in her tracks. Her cry became a gasp. The head servant, who had been listening from outside, had rushed into the room and thrust a sword through her chest.

"He stood over the slain woman, pinning her to the ground with the sword. And a change had come over him. He was transformed. His eyes, which had been cloudy and dark, became clear. He fell onto his knees and begged the old man for forgiveness.

" 'You have acted justly,' said Lazarus. 'Now you must free the girl.'"

"What?" said Aaron. "What girl?"

"I will tell you," said Grandpa Moshe. "That was just the beginning. This is not a story of evil, but of redemption. I will continue. First, could you get me a glass of water?"

Chapter Fourteen

The Rise of Tabitha

Aaron left the room to fill up his water bottle for his grandfather. He looked up and down the garishly bright dorm hallway. The story had made him paranoid. He thought he had heard footsteps, but no one was in sight. Aaron noticed the common room lights were off, which was unusual. Those lights were usually on at all hours, even through the night.

Uneasy, he veered close to the wall as he approached the common room. He reached around the wall to flick on the light switch. But as he groped in the dark, he touched someone. He jumped back and yelled. And someone else yelled.

"Professor Freeman?"

"Aaron! What are you doing here?"

"I live here. What are you doing here?"

"Yes, of course."

Aaron waited for Professor Freeman to go on. He said nothing more. He flicked on the light and turned away.

"What are you doing here?" Aaron repeated.

"I was just, well, you know. I was standing outside your door, listening to your conversation."

"What?" exclaimed Aaron.

"Well, I'm not going to lie to you!"

"How long have you been there?"

"I don't know," said Professor Freeman. "Can I come in?"

"Why were you even here in the first place?"

"I was walking across the quad, and I happened to see your grandfather arrive. I followed him in. Naturally."

Grandpa Moshe appeared in the hallway.

"What's going on?" he called to Aaron.

"Grandpa, Professor Freeman is here."

"What?"

"I just thought I'd stop by," called Professor Freeman from the common room.

"I'm going to fill up my water bottle," said Aaron, shaking his head.

Professor Freeman brought a chair from the common room and set it down in Aaron's dorm room. He crossed his arms and cocked his head at Grandpa Moshe.

"Now what was it you were saying earlier? Something about the Lazarus stuff being nonsense? Something about how I was a real fool?"

"I only take back one of those things," said Grandpa Moshe. "And anyway, I'd say we're even, with all this eavesdropping and sneaking around. We could have you arrested."

"Please don't," said Professor Freeman. "I wouldn't last a day in prison."

"Oh, I know. You wouldn't last an hour. They'd kill you just to shut you up."

Professor Freeman and Aaron sat side by side, across from Grandpa Moshe, who took a drink from the water bottle and sighed.

"Now, listen, Michael," he said. "If you tell a single soul what I say here, I will see that you are murdered by thugs. Do you understand?"

"I certainly do."

Professor Freeman held up his hand to be sworn in. Grandpa Moshe swatted at his hand as he took another drink of water.

"You haven't changed one bit."

"I take that as the highest compliment."

"Anyway," said Grandpa Moshe. "As I was saying, after the head servant had killed Lysbette, Lazarus revealed that he knew about the girl."

"I'm sorry," interrupted Professor Freeman. "Could we pause? Would it be possible to have a brief review? You see, I couldn't hear very well before."

"Michael."

"Okay."

"No."

"I just thought I'd ask, because, you see, I think I missed a few important things. Where did you encounter Lazarus?"

"Michael. No."

"Okay."

Professor Freeman closed his eyes and pursed his lips and nodded quickly. Grandpa Moshe sighed and shook his head.

"So. As I said, Lazarus told the head servant to free the girl. Now, of course, when the head servant heard mention of the girl, he was stricken dumb with horror and shame. Not a soul knew of the girl. Not even the other workers were aware of the girl, although they were accomplices in the genocide.

" 'What am I to do with her?' said the head servant.

" 'Bring her to her family.'

" 'And what am I to do?'

" 'Leave this place.'

"The head servant fell to his knees and begged Lazarus to let him come with him. He pleaded, taking Lazarus by the hand. Lazarus solemnly shook his head. He stood up from the table and went to the door.

" 'Repent of your sins,' he said. 'I am not your judge.'

"Lazarus closed the massive door of the estate house, leaving the head servant alone with his guilt. He knew he could not delay. Tying a cloth over his face, the head servant went into the cellars of the house, to a tiny chamber, hardly large enough for a dog. He undid the lock on the barred wooden door. A small, ragged girl scrambled away in terror. The head servant bent down and held out his open palms to her, begging through tears for her forgiveness. He gathered her up in his arms—she was no more than skin and bones—and brought her up from the cellars. He carried the petrified girl several miles into the town.

"When he arrived in the streets, people came out to see. The head servant wept as he walked, and cried out in repentance, wailing over his sinfulness. The townspeople looked on in confusion, baffled by the scene. Some tried to interfere, to find out what was happening, to help. But the head servant would not stop to explain. He was bent on obeying his orders from Lazarus.

"He walked on through the town, and the commotion grew, until a trail of townspeople had formed behind him. When at last he arrived at the gates of the estate on the far side of town, a crowd surrounded him. He refused to go through the gates. He shouted in tearful desperation, asking the people of the house to come out.

"At last, the Baron van Hofstede himself appeared at the doors of the mansion with his manservant. The two figures walked out along the stone path, across the vast lawns of the estate. They stopped at the gate, confused and appalled by the wretched man, who seemed to be delivering a corpse to their doorstep.

" 'Please, take her!' pleaded the head servant. 'Take the child of Lysbette van Slecht! Take your grandchild!'

"The baron swung open the gate, and the manservant took the small girl in his arms. Lysbette's head servant immediately collapsed, unconscious. He could not be awoken. The townspeople carried him back into the town to be nursed. He remained paralyzed, catatonic, and could not be revived. He lay motionless on a cot, a breathing corpse."

"How?" asked Aaron. "How was he in a coma?"

"Stricken by his sin," murmured Professor Freeman.

Grandpa Moshe shrugged and put up his palms.

"For all that modern science has taught us, there are still many things we don't know," Professor Freeman said.

"What happened to the girl?" said Aaron.

"Yes, the girl," said Grandpa Moshe. "As your professor said, there are many things we do not know. We have many things yet to discover. We might think that a girl kept rotting in a cage for years and years could never recover. How could a person who had undergone so much psychological trauma during such a fundamental period of development ever become healthy? As an honest psychologist would have to admit—and I am one—a truly normal life for anyone who had experienced what she had experienced would be a miracle. Anything more than incremental improvement would be an achievement. And yet, the human spirit is miraculous. We all know this. And I know this firsthand from the camps.

"They carried the girl back into the house, attempting to make sense of the circumstances. They knew nothing of a child. For months after the death of the marquis, no one had seen Lysbette, but they had never for a moment imagined the possibility that she was carrying his child. Lysbette's murderousness, which had otherwise known no bounds, had not extended to her own blood. She had been incapable of destroying her own child. Instead, she had kept her locked in the basement, surviving on filthy water and the most meager scraps from her table.

"The baron was in shock. The existence of this granddaughter in itself was astounding; the hopeless condition of the girl was overwhelming. He instructed his manservant to place the girl in bed. The servants immediately informed the baroness, who hurried to the bedside. When she laid eyes on the shriveled girl, she was speechless. She physically could not utter a sound, and her mind was a blur. After a long time fretting over the girl, she finally managed to speak.

" 'What is your name?'

"The girl only shook her head. She had no name.

" 'You will be Tabitha,' said the baroness. 'For you have overcome death.'"

"Wait," said Aaron.

"Not now," said Grandpa Moshe, giving Aaron a stern look.

"What?" said Professor Freeman.

"Who is Tabitha?" asked Aaron.

"New Testament," said the professor. "Book of Acts. Peter raised her from the dead."

"From that moment," Grandpa Moshe continued, "the entire household staff was summoned to action, and from that day no task became more important than nursing the poor girl Tabitha back to health. Every day, the baron and the baroness ate their meals with the girl. They read to her. They prayed by her bedside. Most importantly, they brought her outside. For long hours in the late summer and early fall, she sat on a reclining chair overlooking the gardens, taking in the sun and the air.

"The resilience of the child was astonishing. Within a matter of months, although still shy and fragile, she was participating in the full life of the household. She was given the existence of a child of privilege. Each day, she spent hours with a tutor, who began teaching her to read and write. At the same time, she had lessons in music, and instruction in painting. They gave her everything they could to help nourish her soul. By the following spring, she was transformed into a dazzling child, eager and grateful. She frolicked across the grounds of the estate, a beautiful small bird freed from a cage.

"As the years passed, the baron and baroness bathed their new heiress in all the love and luxuries they could offer. They spared no expense. She had intricate jewelry and dresses made from the finest materials. They treated her not as a baroness, but as a princess. And no one could have been more deserving, for she never lost the gratitude of being rescued from the bowels of hell, and she never lost the sublime joy of being alive and free.

"At the same time, as she grew older, Tabitha increasingly showed a side of piety. She was often somber and introspective. She was acutely aware of the gift she had been given and was tormented by a sense that she was undeserving. Approaching womanhood, she became more and more devout in her religious observation. She was at the cathedral throughout the week, and spent hours in prayer and reflection. She took to wearing simpler, more subdued clothes, and set aside her jewelry. Once a month, she went to the bedside of the catatonic head servant, the man who had kept her captive. She offered up her forgiveness and prayed for his recovery.

"The baron and baroness realized that to their blossoming granddaughter the wider world held little interest. They had hoped to introduce Tabitha into the company of nobles, to travel with her to the burgeoning cities in the region, but they understood that she was not made for the life of society.

"One day Tabitha went to her grandparents. She asked to go to where she was born, where Lysbette had kept her under lock and key. The baron and the baroness protested. They had sworn never to return to the estate, which had been left to decay. They reminded Tabitha of the horrors that had taken place, of what they had found there after Lysbette's death. In the basement, where Lysbette had kept Tabitha prisoner, they had found a veritable catacomb. The remains of almost a hundred victims of Lysbette's genocide had been stacked against the walls, and on shelves, and in shallow graves beneath the earthen floor.

"But Tabitha persisted. She was intent on returning to the evil place. Unbeknownst to her grandparents, Tabitha had determined her vocation. She had seen a vision of what she must do. When she spoke to them, her voice was full of faith and authority.

" 'What has been a house of the Devil,' she said, 'will be a house of the Lord.'"

Chapter Fifteen

The Order of Tabitha

"The baron and baroness van Hofstede knew they could not stand in Tabitha's way. They decided they had to do all they could to help her. The following day, accompanied by laborers from their own estate, Tabitha and her grandparents returned to the property where the marquis and Lysbette had begun their married life together. They found the house in total disrepair. Windows were broken, and furniture torn to pieces for firewood. Intruders had looted the house, taking silverware from the drawers and pictures from the walls. The lawns and gardens and farm fields were reclaimed by nature, beyond recognition.

"That very day, the servants began the work alongside Tabitha. The baron and baroness begged her not to dirty her hands, but she would not listen. No work was below her. For days, and then weeks, and then months, the work went on. They stripped the house bare. The sprawling upstairs rooms they divided into small, simple cells. In the grand hall, they brought down the chandelier and removed the decorative woodwork from the walls, transforming the space into an austere chapel with rows of hard wooden benches. Against one wall, they built a recent invention: a bookshelf, climbing up to the ceiling, for holy scriptures and ancient texts and a fashionable new technology called printed books.

"They also set to work on the quarters for the laborers, which were on the verge of collapse. Nature had overrun the series of small, connected outbuildings. Wild vines covered the inside and outside of the structures, and saplings grew up among them and within them. Tabitha and the workers cleared away all the overgrowth. They straightened the shelters, reinforced the walls, and replaced the roofs. Finally, they built a small house, apart from the other outbuildings.

"When they had finished the work on the house and the laborers' quarters, Tabitha sent away all the workers. Again, the baron and the baroness protested. They sent the workers back to her. Tabitha would not take them. She even refused to accept any servants for the household, including her own maidservant, who had cared for her from the beginning. Tabitha explained that she was committing herself to doing the will of God; she was devoting her life to service, and so she could not possibly accept the service of another. The maidservant left in tears.

"The next day, Tabitha answered a knock at the door. Her maidservant had returned. She wore a drab black robe, a habit in the style of Tabitha's clothes. Tabitha understood immediately. The two women embraced, as two women equal in God's eyes, no longer restricted by the laws of men. Tabitha welcomed her into the house and showed her to a cell on the second floor. She was the first member of the order.

"Over the next months, word of what was happening spread quickly, creating a great stir in the town. Many thought Tabitha was truly mad. Some even started rumors that she intended to carry out the evil schemes of her mother Lysbette. But most were moved by Tabitha's actions, and admiration for her godly ambitions grew. The townspeople saw that she was giving up all of her privilege, all the comforts of the leisure class. In fact, esteem and wonder exploded, especially among the young women of the town. Families had to discourage their daughters from flocking to Tabitha's doors.

"News spread beyond the town, too, into the surrounding villages and countryside, all the way to the nearest cities. Women of all ages made the journey to Tabitha's doors, performing pilgrimages. Within a year, all the small rooms in the estate house were full. And still women came. They walked for days merely to touch Tabitha's hand, to kneel in the chapel.

"A day at a time, the women of Tabitha's house restored the rest of the property. They tamed the wild yards and planted flowers in the gardens. In the first year, they cultivated one small portion of the fields, growing vegetables and lettuce and herbs to sustain the household. The harvest was abundant. The next year, they expanded the fields, reclaiming the vast tracts of land of the original estate. The women spent all their hours in prayer and reflection and labor, and they only took what they absolutely needed. They lived on small helpings of the great abundance of their harvests. The rest of the food, they carried not only into the town, but into the countryside, and into the nearby villages, doing all they could to feed the hungry.

"In the meantime, during the first years, the quarters for the laborers remained vacant, prepared for the fulfillment of Tabitha's vision. Tabitha waited on the Lord, not on her own timing, praying every day for guidance. Each morning and evening, she opened the front door of the house, hoping for the sign she was anticipating. Each time the sign was not there, she thanked God again for the provisions of the household, and she promised to wait patiently.

"One day, toward the end of the summer, as the harvest approached, when the evening meal had concluded, Tabitha went to the grand entrance, as she always did. She opened the door and fell to her knees in tears. The sign she had been expecting had appeared. A weathered man with a gray beard stood at her doorstep.

" 'Please,' said the man, 'forgive me.'

"Lysbette's head servant, Tabitha's captor, was resurrected. He had woken from his coma and wandered to the estate.

"Tabitha fed him and clothed him, giving him the robes of a laborer, which she had sewn with her own hands. She brought him out to the quarters for the laborers, showing him to the small house, separate from the other outbuildings—the small house she had specially prepared for him. But the head servant refused to go inside. Instead, he asked to be brought to the other shelters. He kissed Tabitha's hand and lay down on a cot, among the other cots.

"Just as Tabitha's maidservant had become the first of many members of her household, so Lysbette's head servant became the first of many laborers. From that day forward, Tabitha opened the doors to those in need of work, and in need of nourishment. Once again, Jews who had been barred from other trades, and old men who had lost their way, and even reformed criminals came to the estate from all across the region. Tabitha and the other women made clothes for all those who came to their door. By the following year, all the cots had occupants, and men had squeezed into the small house built for the head servant.

"And so," said Grandpa Moshe, "Tabitha's vision was complete, her order established."

"No!" blurted out Professor Freeman. "It can't be! But it must be."

Grandpa Moshe blinked slowly as he nodded his head.

"The Order of Tabitha."

"What's that?" said Aaron.

"What would you call it?" asked Professor Freeman. "A sect? A cult?"

Grandpa Moshe shook his head.

"A secret society?"

"I would not call it anything other than its name," said Grandpa Moshe. "The story of the order speaks for itself, and I have not yet finished telling you what Lazarus told us."

Chapter Sixteen

This House Belongs to the Lord

"The Order of Tabitha," said Grandpa Moshe, "was unique. I know of no other religious group of any sort that can compare. Of course, you can say it was a kind of monastic order, and certainly the model was similar to many other abbeys or monasteries, most of which were founded well before Tabitha was born, some even many centuries before. But not one of them survived in the way that the Order of Tabitha survived.

"Yes, as I said, news of what was happening on that estate in Flanders spread far and wide. The name of Tabitha became famous. Over the years, thousands and thousands of pilgrims came to her door. Some stayed only for a short time, and some lived on the estate for the rest of their lives, but only those on the estate who had taken the oath were considered the Order of Tabitha. That was exactly how Tabitha had conceived her vision. The community never grew, in any way, beyond its original realization.

"You see, the Order of Tabitha, no doubt could have exploded, just as the Benedictines and the Dominicans and the Franciscans had exploded, and just as the Jesuits would explode—if Tabitha had allowed it. She had every opportunity. They could have easily expanded the property. They had more than enough laborers and women. Bordering properties attempted to give their land to the estate. Tabitha would not consider for a moment extending the original property lines. They had no reason to have even an inch more land, for God had ordained this one plot of land, and nothing more.

"Nearly every day, pilgrims attempted to leave money and other donations at the estate. Wealthy members of the town and of other towns across the region promised money in their wills. Tabitha never accepted a dime. She sent away the donors, just as she had sent away the servants. To all those who would give their money to her, she told to give their money to those in true need. She assured them that they were in want of nothing, for God provided them all the riches they needed.

"Then, as you can imagine, many begged Tabitha to go out into the world, to spread the message of forgiveness and redemption. Pilgrims asked her to visit their towns. Representatives from distant churches appeared at her door, inviting her to speak to them. She always smiled and shook her head. She was no preacher. She felt no need to speak, for God spoke to each person according to each person's need.

"Those were the doctrines that were laid out for the Order of Tabitha, but not in any codified way. The rules of the community were not inscribed on stone tablets. There was no charter etched in gold on some great scroll. None of Tabitha's words was even recorded on paper. She forbade her followers from keeping histories of what happened at the estate, warning them against the sins of idolatry. All that was remembered during her life was kept safely in the minds of those who lived out the Order of Tabitha."

"Remarkable," said Professor Freeman.

"But wait," said Aaron. "I don't understand."

"I will get there," said Grandpa Moshe. "Be patient."

"Okay."

"Now the only reason that anyone today knows of the Order of Tabitha is one great act of the twentieth century."

"Right," nodded Professor Freeman. "This is the part I know about."

"But as I have said, before that, we do well to keep in mind how amazing was the survival of this small order on this plot of land in Flanders. When Tabitha died, she left nothing at all behind to secure the property. She left no will, and no directions. She did not give any indication that she expected the work to go on. She passed down only what her loyal followers had gleaned from so many days in her presence. Tabitha had understood simply that she had been called to give her life to a divine plan. Once her days were done, her work was complete.

"Hers was an extraordinary life, indeed, but the lives of the women who continued the endeavor are nearly as extraordinary. The anonymous women who carried on the Order of Tabitha for generation after generation deserve all our admiration."

Grandpa Moshe paused and held up a finger.

"You must consider that closely: a human entity, or organization, or society, or whatever you want to call it, that survives without a shred of documentation, without any documents at all! We cannot possibly overestimate what they accomplished. Century after century, they survived, without so much as a simple set of written rules. They did not fight. They had no battles over inheritance and succession. It was a utopia! The faith and righteousness of these women is like nothing else in history. They stayed the course as if Tabitha herself had never died. It is a model to which we all should aspire.

"And that brings us, across nearly half a millennium, through hundreds of years of wars and territorial battles and bloodshed and the emergence of nations, to the events of the twentieth century, to the little-known story of the Order of Tabitha. Maybe, Aaron, you can guess where this tale is going, from the horrors of Lysbette van Slecht to the miracle of the Order of Tabitha. As I said, this is a story full of sadness, and full of hope.

"And this is also some history you should know," said Grandpa Moshe. "Let's see how well your professors have taught you. When did Hitler come to power?"

"1933?" said Aaron.

"That's right. Ten years after the Beer House Putsch. And five years before what?"

"The annexation of Austria."

"Very good. Anschluss. And what else?"

"Kristallnacht," said Professor Freeman.

"I wasn't testing you, but very good."

"Old habits."

"Yes, the Night of Broken Glass," said Grandpa Moshe. "But the war on the Jews had begun well before that. How far back can you say, really? Those with a bad feeling had been quietly leaving Germany for a long time. Some, those with means, fled far off, to the United States. Others, those with less, went where they could. Similar to their ancestors in search of work, in search of a place to live without persecution, they simply packed their things and wandered away, in a sense, desperate for refuge.

"And some fled the continent, leaving everything they had, only to be turned away at the gates. This is a piece of history that you may not know about. In the same year that Germany invaded Poland . . . which was what year?"

"1939," said Aaron.

"Correct. In 1939, a certain ocean liner called the St. Louis left the port of Hamburg carrying nearly a thousand Jews, seeking safe haven. It is one of the saddest stories, representative of so many lost opportunities. The ship first landed in Havana, the intended destination, only to find that the Cubans had changed their laws, revoking the ship's permission to land. A handful of fortunate souls were able to disembark there, but the rest were forced to sail on, in search of refuge elsewhere. Of course, where did they go next?"

"Here?"

"That's right. They sailed to these very shores, up from Havana to Florida. But our Americans had no more of a heart than the Cubans. The American people wanted nothing to do with war in Europe, and nothing to do with the riffraff coming in. You must remember that the ideas so fundamental to the rise of the Nazis—ideas about pure blood and superior races—was by no means restricted to Germans. Roosevelt and his ministers had no reason to cause a scandal—no, not with an election coming up.

"The ship sailed on, headed next for Nova Scotia, where a couple of saintly men had been working to get them entry. In the end, the Canadians were no different from the Americans or the Cubans. They blocked the gate and sent the doomed passengers on. The captain had run out of options, and the accommodations on the ship were deteriorating by the day. Food was becoming scarce. What had begun in Hamburg as a comfortable passage across the Atlantic had become an oceanic death march back to the continent.

"The captain refused to go back to where they had come, however. Whatever it took, he was determined to get his passengers anywhere but Nazi Germany. The ship landed back in Antwerp, with the original passenger list nearly intact. From there, some of the passengers were at last given refuge. Chamberlain accepted hundreds of refugees, who travelled on steamers from Antwerp. The rest were finally allowed to disembark in Antwerp, where the nearby countries accepted them. By the hundreds, they made their way into France, the Netherlands, and, of course, there into Belgium.

"Ah, but the work of the captain to avoid returning to Germany was to be undone, for the borders of the Nazi empire were soon to extend far beyond Germany. The Nazis had already annexed Austria, and just a few months after the St. Louis landed in Antwerp, they marched into Poland. Not long after that, they moved west.

"Another history question," said Grandpa Moshe. "When did the Nazis invade Belgium?"

"1940?"

"Correct again. The Nazi blitzkrieg was as quick as advertised. They were in the Netherlands, Belgium and France by the spring of 1940, and they stayed there until the end of the war. As they did everywhere, they rounded up Jews as they went. So many Jews who hoped they had escaped the jaws of death were snatched back up by the claws of the Reich. Nearly one thousand passengers, full of relief, boarded the St. Louis to escape the Nazis. And do you know how many got away? Only half. Nearly half were victims of the Holocaust.

"Of course, that leaves the half that were blessed enough to survive. Those who landed back on the continent were thrown into the wild scramble to survive. They sought out underground groups and secret safe houses. They did whatever they could, and many were the beneficiaries of charitable individuals, or families, or bigger networks committed to providing protection. Rumors circulated across Europe about safe havens of all sorts, from small family homes, where Jews hid in the walls and floors, to bigger enterprises. Some people committed their lives to smuggling Jews out of Germany and into hiding.

"As Jews sought out safety, word spread of an estate in what was once Flanders, in the Belgian countryside. I can see you've put it together, of course. Just as desperate Jews had once fled to Lysbette van Slecht's estate in hopes of finding work, again desperate Jews fled to the same plot of land, this time in hopes of finding a hiding place. But instead of meeting their death at the hands of an evil woman, they were greeted with open arms by the righteous women of the Order of

Tabitha. Over the course of the war, hundreds of Jews were housed on the estate, in the quarters for the laborers, and in the cells of the convent, and even in the basement, where the corpses of Lysbette's victims had once lain.

"But then, finding a hiding place was only part of the battle. All across Europe, houses suspected of keeping Jews were routinely torn apart, and Tabitha's estate was by no means off the beaten path. In fact—and this is one of the amazing pieces of the story—the road running directly alongside the estate became one of the chief Nazi transport routes. Day after day, troops marched up and down the road, and supply trucks rumbled back and forth. Even tanks and artillery vehicles regularly rolled through. It was a Nazi thoroughfare!

"The women on the estate knew well that they had no way of hiding the hundreds of men, women and children who had found their way to them. The whole group could not even fit in the basement, even if the basement had been a sufficient place to keep them. Instead, they did what they always did, and what the Order of Tabitha had always done: they put their faith in the Lord. Instead of staying holed up in shelters, they carried on the life of the property and prayed for protection. Even the most devout would doubt their logic, and might even accuse them of breaking the commandments by testing the Lord, but their faith swept aside all questioning.

"Inevitably, very early on in the German occupation, the land caught the eye of Nazi officers. The property seemed to be in full operation, teeming with laborers. Not only would the estate be a place to supply food for their troops, but a perfect house for the officers—a home fit for the military brass. And sadly, I need not mention, men being what they are, that a house full of women would have likewise been an attraction.

"One afternoon, in the summer of 1940, two officers, accompanied by a unit of troops, approached the grand entrance. A woman in a drab black robe, and a black head covering, answered the door. The officer peered beyond her, into the house. He could see the bare chapel, which had been the grand hall, and the impressive collection of old books on one of the walls. He was not deterred. He went through the customary announcement, making clear that the estate, as well as all surrounding areas, from that point forward, was at the disposal of the Reich.

"Now," said Grandpa Moshe, "before I continue, I must warn you that you should not be ready for some dramatic event. If you expect that every confrontation between the Nazis and the forces of resistance must end in explosive action, you have seen too many films. In a movie, a squadron of nuns would appear in the windows with Uzis and mow down the whole unit of Nazis as the woman at the door peacefully watched. Then they would drag all the bodies into the basement, and when another unit of Nazis came along, they would do the same. No, no, that is not the case. Sometimes the most miraculous and exciting events happen without any great commotion whatsoever.

"When the officer had finished his long preamble, and had asserted in very plain language, so as not to be misunderstood, that the house belonged to them, the woman at the door was prepared to answer confidently.

" 'I'm sorry,' said the woman, kind and yet assertive, 'but you are mistaken. This house belongs to the Lord.'

"The officer was accustomed to protests of all types, even the exact response that the woman had offered. They had occupied other religious properties along the way, using them for various purposes. Somehow, though, this response was different, and the voice of the woman was different. The officer was taken aback, and found he could not speak. He was at a loss. More than that, he must have sensed that he was standing on holy ground. To the bewilderment of the other officer, and to the unit of troops, the officer merely nodded and turned, almost in a stupor.

"But that is not the most incredible part of the story. What happened next is perhaps even more astounding, and what happened next is nothing at all. For the duration of the war, not a single Nazi soldier stepped on the estate. They seemed to make a point of avoiding the property. An understanding grew among the troops and officers that the land was sacred land, not to be defiled in any way. No food was to be taken, and no person to be touched.

"Once again, and in some ways more perfectly than ever before, Tabitha's vision was fulfilled, and Lysbette's evil was reversed. The estate was a refuge for Jews and others deemed undesirable by the Nazis. And just as the townspeople had once avoided Lysbette out of fear of her wickedness, the Nazis avoided the Order of Tabitha out of fear of their godliness."

Grandpa Moshe stopped, allowing the words to settle. Professor Freeman very softly pressed his palms together, offering a quiet applause.

"Fascinating," said Professor Freeman.

Aaron nodded.

"He's not a bad storyteller, eh?" said Professor Freeman. "Now you see where I get it."

"You didn't get that from me."

"Is that the last thing Lazarus said?" asked Aaron.

"Not quite. There is still more to tell," said Grandpa Moshe. "But not before bed."

Both Aaron and Professor Freeman, who had gradually inched forward, hanging on every word, slumped back in their chairs.

"I'm sorry, boys. An old man has to sleep. I can start again in the morning."

Professor Freeman slapped his knees and stood up.

"It is nearing midnight," he agreed. "You must come stay with me. I have ample space."

"No, no, no," said Grandpa Moshe. "I'll be fine here. I'm practically falling over."

"This is absurd. I can't have my esteemed professor spending the night in a dorm when he could sleep in a proper bed at my home."

"Please."

"By the way, you really should see my home. You'll be comfortable, I promise. Wages have really improved since your day."

"Michael. That's enough."

At last, Grandpa Moshe was able to push Professor Freeman out the door, but not without one final pronouncement on his profound disgust that his venerable former professor should spend the night in such squalor.

"And," said Professor Freeman, as Grandpa Moshe closed the door on him, "you better not continue without me!"

Grandpa Moshe locked the door and leaned up against it with a sigh.

"He's exhausting. How do you put up with him? He doesn't care where I sleep. He just doesn't want to miss any of the story!"

"That's exactly what I was thinking," said Aaron.

"Sucker," said Grandpa Moshe. "Of course we're going to continue without him. It's barely after eleven. And now I can answer the question I saw forming on your lips. But can I have some more water first? All this talking has me parched."

Aaron left to refill his water bottle in the bathroom. When he returned, his grandfather was lying on top of the blankets of his twin bed, sound asleep. Aaron pulled out the futon and turned out the lights.

Chapter Seventeen

Agata's Silent Farewell

"Aaron," whispered Grandpa Moshe. "Aaron."

Aaron shuffled and turned over. He blinked in the darkness. Grandpa Moshe was stumbling across the room, feeling out the furniture. Aaron put up his arms to protect himself.

"Aaron? Are you awake?"

"Yeah, Grandpa. I'm awake."

"I have to go to the bathroom. I almost peed myself. Where's the door?"

Aaron pulled off his blankets and sat up on the futon. He stood up with his arms extended, feeling around for his grandfather. They quickly found each other.

"Ah, there you are, old friend. Can you switch on the light before I break my neck?"

Once he had pointed his grandfather in the direction of the bathroom, Aaron collapsed on the futon and rubbed his eyes. He was falling back asleep sitting up when his grandfather, quite awake, returned to the room.

"I fell asleep there," said Grandpa Moshe. "One of the perils of old age. It can happen any time. The sleep fairy stopped using fairy dust on me a long time ago. Now she hits me over the head with one of those gigantic carnival hammers."

Aaron nodded sleepily.

"Are you awake or what?"

"Sort of," said Aaron.

"We should keep going with the story. You know that professor of yours is going to be back here with a tray of coffees at the crack of dawn. I don't want to tell that fool about my personal life. Plus, there are a few things he really can't know. Do you remember that thing you were going to ask me?"

"Yeah, well, I had a couple things. Obviously, my ears perked up when you mentioned the name Tabitha."

"Of course."

"But I don't fully understand. Did your wife join the Order of Tabitha?"

"That's where it gets a bit complicated. That wouldn't make sense, if you remember."

"Right. That's what I thought. How could she be in the Order of Tabitha when the Order of Tabitha only existed on that one plot of land."

"Exists," said Grandpa Moshe.

"Really?" said Aaron.

"But that's another story. Anyway, that's exactly what I was thinking as I sat in that dark room buried beneath the city of Lodz as Lazarus told us about the Order of Tabitha. The whole time I listened to him, I had to assume that my wife had joined this society, or whatever you want to call it. It made perfect sense. She was living in a household of women, all dressed in black, the same way he described Tabitha's original group. Like Tabitha, these women, too, had risen from the dead, in a sense. My wife, Agata, had been starved and tortured in the camps, just as the girl had suffered in her tiny chamber in the basement of Lysbette's estate house. But there was that one problem, impossible to resolve."

"How could she be in the Order of Tabitha if she did not live on that plot of land?"

"Exactly," said Grandpa Moshe. "She could not be. Unless, of course, something had changed, if the unwritten rules, codified over centuries in the faithfulness of these women, had somehow been rewritten."

"Did you ask her?"

"Did I ask her," said Grandpa Moshe. "Did I ask her. No, I did not ask her."

Grandpa Moshe dropped his head. He let out a rueful whistle and wiped at the corner of his eye with the tip of his finger.

"After Lazarus had left, the group of women, who were all seated in the front of the audience, filed out in one line before everyone else. I could not even see which one she was. I could only guess. I'm sure she would have wanted it that way, to be anonymous, indistinguishable from all her sisters.

"I waited for everyone else to leave from their rows. In the row in front of me, an old man, a rabbi, shuffled into the aisle. I patted him on the arm.

" 'That group of women,' I asked. 'Is that the Order of Tabitha?'

"The old man frowned and shook his head.

" 'Who are they?' I asked.

" 'That is not the Order of Tabitha,' he told me, 'but each is named Tabitha.'

"The rabbi left me with that head-scratcher. He said nothing else. Typical rabbi, right?"

"You never got to ask her?" said Aaron.

"No, I never got to ask her. Never again would they answer my knock at the door. I never once saw my beloved Agata again."

"I'm sorry."

Grandpa Moshe stood up weakly with his head bowed. He inched toward the bed.

"I think I'm finally ready to sleep," he said.

Aaron got up to help him, but Grandpa Moshe waved him away without looking at him. Aaron watched his grandfather pull off the sheets and climb into bed. When he was situated, Aaron switched off the light. The two lay quietly. As Aaron began to doze, he heard his name—a voice in the fog.

"Aaron," said Grandpa Moshe.

"Yeah," mumbled Aaron.

"That note—the one on the picture."

"Yeah."

"I didn't write that note, Aaron."

Chapter Eighteen

The Parable of the Prince

Aaron woke up with a start. He sensed he had been dreaming. He turned onto his side, and his ears perked up. A soft knock came at the door. Aaron wiped his face and stood up. His grandfather was still asleep. He opened the door a crack. Just as Grandpa Moshe had predicted, an eager Professor Freeman was on the other side, holding a tray of coffees.

"Are you still not awake?" he hissed. "I've been waiting out here for an hour!"

"What time is it?"

"It's after seven!"

"I thought you weren't a morning person?"

"I'm not above exceptions . . ."

"He's still sleeping," whispered Aaron. "I'm not going to wake him up."

Professor Freeman huffed.

"I'll get you as soon as he's up."

Aaron gently closed the door on his scowling professor. He sat back down on the futon. Grandpa Moshe raised his head and opened one eye. He held out a fist from the blankets and popped his thumb up.

An hour later, Grandpa Moshe and Aaron emerged from the dorm room, dressed for the day. They found Professor Freeman in the common room, dozing on a couch. Grandpa Moshe took a cold coffee from the tray on the table. He nudged Professor Freeman.

"Got any cream for this?"

"Get away!" said Professor Freeman.

He spastically sat up and batted at the air. Grandpa Moshe flinched and stepped back.

"Oh," said the professor. "It's you. You're awake. I was fighting off a man with a scimitar in the streets of Alexandria. He almost got me, too."

"Quite a dream life," said Grandpa Moshe. "You ready for some breakfast?"

"Yes. I know just the place, not too far."

Professor Freeman led Grandpa Moshe and Aaron to his favorite table in the back corner of the campus coffee shop.

"They have excellent breakfast sandwiches," said Professor Freeman. "I recommend the egg whites and spinach."

"What on earth?" said Grandpa Moshe with a grimace.

He looked at Aaron with a mix of disbelief and disgust. Aaron shrugged and smirked.

"It really is quite good," said Professor Freeman. "What can I get you?"

"I'll take anything with bacon and yolks," said Grandpa Moshe. "Some cheese would be great, too."

"That'd be great for me, too," said Aaron. "Thank you."

They settled into their seats at the table as Professor Freeman went back to the counter to order the food. Grandpa Moshe leaned across the table, keeping an eye on Professor Freeman.

"Don't say anything about Agata," said Grandpa Moshe.

Aaron nodded.

"Or the note."

"Does mom know about what happened in Poland?"

"Yes."

"But I thought you said you hadn't told anyone else."

"Of course. That's what you always say if you want someone to keep a secret."

Professor Freeman returned with coffees and napkins.

"So," he said. "Shall we continue?"

"You know something? You're even more eager now than you were as a student."

"What do you expect? This is more important than anything. Ever."

"That's what concerns me. I want you to make an actual promise."

"Yes?" said Professor Freeman.

"You're not to tell a soul about any of this."

"I promise."

"And," said Grandpa Moshe. "I better not see this story among a bunch of other crappy thrillers in some airport book shop."

"You have my word."

"I'll have your head if you don't keep it. Let's go on. I finished the Lysbette story, right?"

"Right," said Aaron.

"So that was the last—and probably the most memorable—story Lazarus told us that evening. However, it wasn't the last thing he told us.

"When he had finished the tale of the Order of Tabitha, he said, 'All you have heard here this evening is the truth. I have given you the facts of a history never recorded. But now I will leave you with a parable.'"

"Oh, dear," said Professor Freeman. "I have shivers."

"This," said Grandpa Moshe, "is what he told us. Long ago, before the lands of the earth had formed, rumor spread far and wide of a young man more handsome and more prosperous than any young man in all the world. His eyes were more beautiful than the ocean. His hair was like a field of golden grain before the harvest. He was also a strong man. He felled trees in the forest and plowed his own fields. He was a man among men. He owned all the hills as far as the eye could see, as far as the mountains to the north and the seas to the south. And he was known for his high moral standing. He was generous and kind.

"More important than all these things, this rumored young man was said to know all there was to know. His intelligence was beyond all measure. He was a master of all knowledge. Whenever anyone had a question of great importance, the wisdom of the young man was sought.

"But what was most remarkable about this young man, this prince, was that no one had ever seen him. They had heard of his wonderful appearance. They had seen the signs of the abundance of his wealth. His palatial, rambling properties were a testament to his prominence. His wise sayings were promulgated far and wide. His advice, to those who begged his counsel, was delivered in written decree or verbal notice by the servants who managed his household. In short, the identity of the prince was a great mystery.

"Now it came to be that the prince determined that he must have a mate. And so—as you have come to expect from any fairy tale—all the royal houses across the known world prepared to make an appeal to the young man. Almost every day, a new suitor arrived, determined to find favor with the prince. But—again as you have come to expect from any fairy tale—no suitor seemed to be suitable.

"That is not to say, however, that each suitor was not given a fair chance at winning the heart of the prince. In fact, according to all those who visited the grounds, he had established an elaborate system for vetting his potential brides. Any woman who wished to present herself to the prince had to pass a series of tests administered by the servants of the household.

"In the first test, a woman was given entry to one of the many libraries of the household. In the middle of the room would be stacks of manuscripts and other documents. For three days, the woman was to remain in this library. No other instruction was given. Meals were served, and proper bedding provided."

"What's the test?" said Aaron. "I don't get it."

"For some, being locked in a library for three days is a test. Maybe for you?"

"Maybe," smiled Aaron.

"In the second test," said Grandpa Moshe, "a woman was given charge of a flock of sheep. For three days, the woman was to care for these sheep. She was to offer them nurture and protection. In the face of nature's perils, of roving predators and dangerous crags and flooding rivers, she was to ensure that all the sheep remained safe.

"This is standard stuff, of course. I need not go into great detail. The tests themselves are not significant."

"But what the tests measure . . ." said Professor Freeman.

"Yes. Perhaps," said Grandpa Moshe. "As you'd expect, very few made it beyond the first test, and fewer still beyond the second test. How many princesses are shepherdesses? Say that five times fast. And, naturally, almost no one made it beyond the third and final test, which was at once the most simple and the most difficult of the three.

"Only a few women among hundreds passed both tests. After the second test, each woman who passed was welcomed by the head servant into an antechamber, which led into the front hall of the palace.

"The servant told each woman, 'Please, take with you all that you wish. Your carriage has been summoned.'

"The servant then opened the door of the antechamber into the magnificent front hall, where all the treasures of the palace were spread out in marvelous array. The heavy, ornate doors to the palace were open for her departure, her carriage waiting. At once, each woman, one after another, was overcome by the sight of the riches. Without hesitation, she plunged into the opulent piles, filling up satchels and boxes of gold and silver and jewels of every kind. With the help of her servants and maids, she loaded every carriage of her entourage with as much of the treasure as she could possibly carry.

"Each woman, that is, except for one. This young woman was not noteworthy in any particular way. Yes, she had passed the first two tests. But she is not the heroine of the story. She did not have a heart of gold, and she was not a pauper disguised as a princess. Nor was she a witch of some sort, as you might anticipate in some other fairy tale. No, she was only exceptional in that she was the lone woman who passed all three tests.

"When the servants opened the door of the antechamber to reveal all the riches tumbling out into the front hall, she scarcely looked. Instead, she turned to the servant.

"The young woman said, 'I am here to see the prince.'

"The servant replied, 'You have passed the final test. You shall see the prince.'

"The servant bowed. He led the young woman at once through many great rooms to the far end of the palace, to the chambers of the prince. The servant left her outside a set of doors. He disappeared, only to return a short while later. He opened the door wide and ushered the young woman into another great hall. Light streamed into the space from tall, lancet windows along either side of the long room. At the far end of the hall, in a shrouded throne, sat the mysterious prince, the young man who had inspired myriad rumors.

" 'You may stop there,' said the servant. 'Please state your name and whence you come.'

The woman, trembling, revealed her name and her homeland. She stood in silence, trying to decipher the shadowy figure of the prince, who sat behind a veil, where the light from the windows could not reach him. After a moment, she saw some vague gesture in the distance, a summoning. The servant immediately paced across the room to the throne. Some exchange occurred, some indistinct whispering. The servant returned to the woman with an envelope that bore the marks of a decree by the prince, whose crest was known throughout the land. He presented the young woman with the envelope, instructing her to deliver it to her parents.

"At that, the servant led the young woman out of the presence of the prince. He brought her again through the many rooms of the palace, back to the antechamber. Again, he told her to take freely from the treasure before leaving. The young woman, too distraught to accept the invitation, went straight to her carriage without so much as a glance at the riches. She mounted her carriage and told her horsemen to ride. She could only assume that the prince had not approved of her appearance. At the same time, she did not dare open the envelope. Imagining that the prince, once more, might be putting her to the test, the young woman held the envelope close. She travelled the entirety of the trip with the unopened decree on her lap.

"After three days, the young woman arrived at the gates of her palace, where her parents had been anxiously awaiting news of her attempt to win the prince's hand. When she entered the palace, they begged her for news. The young woman, weary and overwrought, delivered the envelope to her parents and disappeared to her chambers. Baffled and concerned, her parents weighed the envelope in their hands, passing it back and forth. They recognized immediately the crest of the prince. They hoped, of course, for the acceptance of their daughter, and feared a formal rejection. The envelope contained neither.

"In the handwriting of the prince read a single line. The prince asked a question: 'Why have you sent me your daughter?'

"The king and queen stared aghast at the note, not knowing what to make of it. Their confusion quickly turned to outrage. They assumed the worst, that the prince, who was otherwise known for his nobility of spirit, had sent them an insult of the highest magnitude, questioning the mere idea that they should think their daughter worthy of the prince. For days they raged, and they considered various forms of retribution.

"But when their ire had subsided, they returned to their confusion. The note, if taken as an insult, seemed distinctly out of character, for the prince was known for his uprightness. They decided there had to be more to the note than a cruel, crude insult. They asked neighboring families if they had received any such decree. No one had. Of course, only their daughter had progressed through all three tests. They shared the decree with any who might be able to help them. Many made guesses at the meaning. No one could answer with any authority.

"At last, they determined they must go to the prince himself. As was the custom, they went to the gates of his palace to submit an inquiry. There they waited for the servants of the prince to attend to them. But no one came. The gates were shut forever."

Grandpa Moshe paused as Aaron and Professor Freeman pondered the parable.

"That was the last thing Lazarus told us," concluded Grandpa Moshe. "He stood up and walked out, an apparition."

"Amazing," said Professor Freeman. "But even more amazing when you consider what I am about to tell you."

Grandpa Moshe looked at his watch. He groaned and put his hands on his head, pulling at his thinning white hair.

"What is it?" said Aaron.

"Oh, no," said Grandpa. "Your mother. She has that lecture tonight. I said we'd be there."

"What?"

Grandpa Moshe looked into Aaron's eyes and nudged him with his foot under the table.

"That's right," said Aaron. "I completely forgot."

"It's in a few hours. We have to get on the road."

"Wait! Please," pleaded Professor Freeman. "You really must listen to this. I promise this will not take long."

"Won't take long? From you?" said Grandpa Moshe. "We better go, Aaron."

Grandpa Moshe stood up. Professor Freeman jumped up with him and grabbed his arm.

"Please. I beg you. You must hear this. I may have the key to unlocking the parable."

Grandpa Moshe glared skeptically at Professor Freeman, and gradually sank into his seat.

Chapter Nineteen

The Parable of the Woodworker

"Now," said Professor Freeman, "there is one other thing I never mentioned to you about that day at Princeton, Aaron. In some ways, it didn't seem relevant. That is, until now. After this man who called himself Lazarus had finished telling us those stories, he did exactly as he did that night in Lodz. He left us with a parable."

"You said this would be brief," interrupted Grandpa Moshe. "That was not a brief start."

"I'm sorry. I'll try to be briefer. I have a way, you know, of telling a story."

"Yes, I know that."

"I'll be briefer if you don't interrupt."

Grandpa Moshe rolled his eyes at Aaron.

"The parable he told us was not nearly as long as the one he told you," said Professor Freeman, "but it was just as mysterious, or perhaps even more mysterious. In any case, it was certainly stranger."

Grandpa Moshe glanced at his watch.

"You're ruining this, you know," said Professor Freeman.

"Just tell us the parable, would you!"

"There was a woodworker who lived in a small town," said Professor Freeman. "He was an accomplished craftsman. He had trained well for his work, and his work was prized. He made ornate chairs and armoires for the noble families of the town, and he made sturdy beds and shelves for the common people. All that to say, he was a respected citizen. All those around him held him in high regard."

"You said that already."

"Yes, so! His diligence and ability had afforded him, let's say, a comfortable existence. He was never in want. He had plenty to eat, and his home was secure. Most would say he had achieved contentment. The woodworker himself would have admitted that he had no reason to complain. He could have envied those of the nobility, or those of great learning, but envy was not in his nature.

"And yet, at the very time in which he had achieved what would have seemed to be perfect happiness for his particular circumstances, the woodworker discovered that his life was, in fact, quite empty. To repeat—if you'll so graciously allow—he was not one to complain, and so he did not instinctively examine all the ways his life could be better. He did not bemoan a lack of riches or a lack of important work. He knew he had enough wealth, and he knew his craft served a purpose. What he sought was something more, something beyond practical parameters. He yearned for a deeper meaning, without which all else seemed vacuous.

"Wasting no time, the woodworker packed a bag and shuttered his house. He entrusted his apprentice with his shop and set out on a journey in hopes of discovering the fundamental sense of purpose which he seemed to be missing."

"You are getting close, I hope," said Grandpa Moshe.

"I'm halfway there. I'd be more than halfway if you hadn't interrupted me again," said Professor Freeman. "The woodworker set out to explore the world. He travelled by foot day after day, sleeping under the stars or wherever he could find hospitality. Every place he went, he sought out the wise people of the land. He asked questions, and he listened. And every place he went, they instructed him that he must go to a place called the Great Mountain, where there lived the wisest man the world had ever known.

"After weeks and weeks of traversing the country, the woodworker at last arrived at the foot of the Great Mountain."

"Did he get to the top of the mountain?" said Grandpa Moshe.

"Yes."

"Well, then just skip to that."

"I swear, you are really missing out on this story," said Professor Freeman. "It's a great story. I'm not doing it justice. I can't work in these conditions!"

"We don't have time!"

"I'm almost done. The woodworker climbed to the top of the Great Mountain, doing all sorts of spectacular things along the way, which you will never know about, and at the top he found the wise man seated on a stone. Wise men never need much more than that, you know. The woodworker sat down on the ground across from the wise man, and the wise man gestured for him to speak. The woodworker explained his situation. He described how he had left a very comfortable existence in search of meaning. He told of his journeys.

"The wise man listened in silence, not reacting in any way. When the woodworker had finished telling his story, the wise man spoke.

" 'I have been expecting you,' he said. 'I have prepared for you a path.'

" 'Please,' exclaimed the woodworker, 'show me the path.'

" 'On the other side of this mountain,' said the wise man, 'down at the base, you will find a moat. This moat is too wide to leap, and too dangerous to swim. No person has crossed this moat without assistance. But I have set aside a piece of strong wood for you, the strongest wood that exists in these parts. This is the only type of wood that will serve you in your attempts to cross the moat. If you succeed in crossing the moat, you will understand your purpose.'

"The woodworker bowed and thanked the wise man. Sure enough, on the other side of the mountain, he found the piece of hard wood. The wise man had set aside the trunk of a tree, stripped of all branches, about six inches in diameter on one end, and about an inch in diameter on the other end. The woodworker, a master of his craft, understood immediately that the wood would be very difficult to use. He wasted no time. He explored the mountain, collecting various objects. Using rocks of all sizes, he fashioned cutting tools and mallets. With the cutting tools, he made other tools out of wood and stone.

"I should add . . ." continued Professor Freeman.

"Should you?" asked Grandpa Moshe.

"Yes, I should! I decidedly should add that he delighted in his craft, reveling in the flow of his labor, this being his first time practicing his trade after many months. Okay? That could be important. So there!"

Grandpa Moshe elbowed Aaron.

"In any case, once he had a small collection of tools, he split and cut the piece of wood into smaller pieces, beginning from the thicker end of the trunk. He joined the pieces together into a platform, a raft. Using the thinner end of the trunk, he saved one third of the piece of wood and carved it into a rudimentary oar. Finally, after days and days of diligent labor, the woodworker stood back to admire his work. He had used nearly every inch of the piece of wood set aside for him by the wise man."

"Okay, that's a good stopping place," said Grandpa Moshe. "I'm interested, but we have to go."

Grandpa Moshe pushed his chair out from the table, and Professor Freeman leapt from his seat with his arms outstretched to hold him.

"I'll tell you the rest as we walk," insisted Professor Freeman.

Grandpa Moshe led the way out of the coffee shop, setting off at a near trot. Professor Freeman followed along excitedly, almost jogging beside him. The three of them walked in a tight cluster across the quad.

"The next day," said Professor Freeman, "the woodworker bid farewell to the wise man and began his trek down the other side of the mountain, the burden of the heavy wood raft on his back. Struggling under the weight of the burden, the woodworker slowly traversed the steep, winding path to the foot of the mountain. As he got closer, he could see the moat far below, glistening in the last light of day. The woodworker stopped to sleep for the night, in sight of the moat, which was no more than a thin, shining strip in the distance.

"When he awoke, he hiked down the rest of the mountain, onto the flats, where there was no vegetation for miles. Plodding for hours across the barren land, he at last arrived at the moat, which stretched in either direction as far as he could see. But he was surprised that the moat was not nearly as wide as he had assumed. He imagined that with one very good leap, he might be able to touch the far edge, or at least get close enough to swim to the other side. He had to remind himself of the wise man's words. He stuck his oar into the moat and drew the oar back and forth through the turbid water. The moat was dark and thick, as much mud as water. He could not detect any movement or current.

"Not seeing any reason to delay, he set his tiny raft down on the moat and clambered aboard on his knees, his oar in hand, and pushed off from the edge as best he could."

Professor Freeman stopped. They had reached the edge of the parking lot next to Aaron's dormitory. Aaron hesitated, waiting for his professor to continue. Grandpa Moshe kept walking several paces. He turned around impatiently.

"Yes?" said Grandpa Moshe.

"This is my car," said Professor Freeman.

"You could walk us to our car!"

"That wouldn't make much sense, would it?"

Grandpa Moshe threw up his arms and wandered back over to the car. They stood next to the open car door.

"Can you guess what happened?" said Professor Freeman.

"No," said Grandpa Moshe.

"The raft sinks," said Aaron.

"Precisely!"

"No sooner had the woodworker pushed off into the moat than he realized that the heavy raft was rapidly sinking. The moat was not water at all, but quicksand! In a flash, all the wood he had carefully joined together had disappeared beneath his knees into the murk. He managed to scramble up from his knees onto his feet, but the quicksand was climbing up his legs and had nearly reached his thighs. He stood upright, holding the oar with both hands above his head, frantically searching for anything at all to grab.

"Losing hope, steadily sinking to his grave, the woodworker looked at the rudimentary oar in his hands. Before the quicksand could creep up to his chin, the woodworker understood what a fool he had been. He glanced from one side of the moat to the other, and again examined the piece of wood in his hands. To a man of his expertise, a man of his spatial awareness, honed over many years of woodworking, the solution could not have been more obvious."

"What did he do?" said Aaron.

"He did nothing. It was too late. But he sank beneath the quicksand knowing the simple truth. All his careful work—all his fashioning of tools and cutting of wood and joining of pieces—had been in vain. The wise man had given him what he needed to cross the moat. He needed only to have set down the trunk across the moat and climbed from one side to the other."

"Ha!" said Grandpa Moshe. "But now we really have to leave. Let's go, Aaron."

"You're going with him?" said Professor Freeman. "But we need to figure this out! What do the parables mean?"

"Next weekend," said Grandpa Moshe. "Just relax."

"How am I supposed to relax?"

Professor Freeman was pleading with Grandpa Moshe to stay. Now he followed them to their car. Grandpa Moshe started the engine and rolled down the window. Professor Freeman had worked himself into a tizzy. He was nearly ranting.

"I think I've had it all mixed up!" he said. "I've been thinking about the wrong things. For all these years I've been trying to make sense of the lessons in the parable. And I have no doubt that the lessons are profound. But it isn't about the lessons at all! It's about the moat!"

"I'll be back next weekend."

Grandpa Moshe began to roll up his window. Professor Freeman held his fingers over the window, tugging them away right before the window closed.

"The same with your parable!" Professor Freeman shouted through the car window. "Your parable makes it clear. It isn't about anything in the story at all! The story's a distraction. It's all about the ending!"

Grandpa Moshe smiled pleasantly and waved Professor Freeman off. He put the car in reverse and backed out of the parking spot. Professor Freeman walked alongside the car with his palms upturned. Finally, he threw up his hands, resigned, as Grandpa Moshe slowly pulled away.

"It's about the moat!" he yelled after them.

Grandpa Moshe watched him for a moment in his rearview mirror.

"He was dangerously close to figuring it out," he said. "We need to get out of here."

"Where are we going?" said Aaron.

"I'll tell you on the way," said Grandpa Moshe. "The time has come."

Chapter Twenty

An Old Philosophy Professor Named Marta

Grandpa Moshe did not say a word. He stared through the front windshield, out onto the highway, as if Aaron was not even in the car. Aaron was restless beside him. From time to time, he looked over at his grandfather, waiting for him to speak.

"Grandpa?" said Aaron.

"Yeah."

"Are you okay?"

"I'm okay," said Grandpa Moshe. "I'm just a little tired."

"Do you want me to drive?"

"That's all right, Aaron. I'm managing."

Grandpa Moshe's brow was wrinkled with worry. Aaron watched him expectantly, but did not want to press him.

"You have to understand that all this is a great weight to bear," said Grandpa Moshe. "What I am going to tell you will change you. You won't be the same."

"I think I can handle it."

"I know you can handle it, Aaron. But that doesn't mean I give you this burden gladly. You had to know all this eventually. I just would have rather been able to tell you all this myself, before Michael could get to you. I had no idea he even knew any of this stuff. Not many people have heard these stories. I was hoping to tell you when you were a little older."

"What is it all about?" asked Aaron. "I don't understand."

"There is so much yet to learn," said Grandpa Moshe. "This is just the beginning. And we still have many loose ends."

"The one thing I can't get out of my mind is that you said something about your old philosophy professor. Were you kidding?"

"Ah, yes. That's a good place to pick up," said Grandpa Moshe, taking a deep breath. "You know, of course, that I have always been a student of psychology. Even today, psychology and philosophy are very much intertwined. In my day, that was even more the case. When I was a young man at the university, back in Poland, psychology was almost a branch of philosophy. Now psychology stands on its own two feet.

"When I resumed my studies at Rutgers, I was training as much to be a philosopher as a psychologist, at least in my mind. I took several courses—as many courses as I could—in the philosophy department. My mentor was a Jewish woman from Poland named Marta who had escaped Europe years before the Nazis came to power. She had seen the writing on the wall and gotten out when she could. She had left everything behind, as so many did.

"I could tell from the moment I met Marta that we were cut from the same cloth, and not only because we were both Polish Jews. We were kindred spirits. We also had the same perspective on philosophy, on the world. She grasped immediately all the ideas I was wrestling with during those years, not only in my academic work, but in my life. She was much further along down the same path. She didn't know where the path would end, but she was able to turn back and shine a flashlight on the ground in front of me to help me inch along. That is what a mentorship is.

"She was also brilliant, and I mean that when I say it. Many people throw that term around. These days, professors call half their students brilliant. That's impossible. This was different. I have no doubt in my mind that she was a certified genius. You might not know it because she never did anything to show off her knowledge. Whatever I happened to be telling her about—whatever I was reading at the time—she would know it twice as well, but she never interrupted me or made me feel stupid. She simply knew everything.

"I became very close with Marta. As I said, she was a mentor, and she became more important to me than any of my psychology professors because she became a real friend. When I began to teach at Rutgers, we became colleagues, too. I consulted with her constantly as I navigated the waters of my first few years as a full professor. She had mentored me as a student, and then she mentored me as a professor.

"Almost no one knew of my journey back to Poland, across the Soviet line, in search of Agata. Many would have thought I was insane, and perhaps I was. I had told Marta, however. I had to tell her. When I got back, I was heartbroken, and she could see immediately. I told her what had happened. I told her every detail. That is, I told her about everything except the experience of seeing Lazarus.

"I was shocked to learn that Marta was well-aware of the legend of the Order of Tabitha. In fact, she was able to corroborate many of the details, to help give me a better idea of the group's obscure history. To learn from her about the Order of Tabitha was somehow a great comfort. She helped me to accept that Agata had chosen a noble calling. I considered what had happened in new terms. Over time, I stopped lamenting the loss of my wife. Instead, I found consolation in thinking that I was sacrificing the love of my life so that Agata could fulfill her spiritual calling. In the end, that was the idea that allowed me to move on, to find a new love—ultimately, to marry your grandmother. Marta was also instrumental in that. I will get to that.

"Putting all that aside for now, Marta could sense there was more I was not telling her. She knew that something else was on my mind in those months and years after my journey to Poland. She seemed to know that something else had happened. She was too good a friend not to see it; she was also too good a friend to press me when she saw that I was not ready to speak. Any time my trip to Poland came up, though, she would ask me if anything else had happened, if there was anything else I wanted to say. But she would never press me.

"You can be certain, there were many reasons I didn't want to tell her about the strange meeting with this person who had called himself Lazarus, who had claimed to be the man who had died and come back to life. No part of it made sense. As much as I knew that I could say anything to Marta, I was embarrassed. It was that simple. And I was even more ashamed for the way I wasn't able to let the story go. I should have been able to dismiss the whole thing as nonsense, albeit sophisticated nonsense."

"That's exactly how I've felt," said Aaron.

"Yes, you understand. And I must apologize again for being false when you first showed me the picture. I didn't want you to learn about all this yet."

"It's okay," said Aaron. "I'm ready."

Grandpa Moshe reached across and patted Aaron on the chest.

"Anyway, there came a point when I could no longer resist telling Marta the full story. I invited her to my home so that we could not be disturbed or overheard by anyone, and I told her every last thing I could remember, down to the arid, ancient smell of the underground room in Lodz. I told her about the appearance of Lazarus, about his mystical presence. He was otherworldly. I felt silly telling her these things, but she listened trustingly. As I said, even if she knew each word that came out of your mouth, she would let you tell her. That was the incredible depth of her humility—and of her confidence, you would have to say.

"When I had finished pouring out my story, she said very little. She expressed to me her genuine interest in all I had described, and she thanked me sincerely for sharing. She admitted that she knew something else had been on my mind all those months, and she was honored that I had finally been willing to lay myself bare. She knew that it could not have been easy to make myself vulnerable in that way—deep down we academics are terrified of looking stupid. But that was all she said. I asked for her opinion. I nearly begged her for any sort of reaction. She told me she would dwell on all these things, that she needed time to digest all I had said. She left me there in my home, feeling very alone.

"A few days passed, and still I heard nothing from Marta. I did not see her on campus. I even walked by her office a few times, and she was never there. As much as I tried not to be paranoid, I could not avoid the thought that I had lost my mentor, my friend. I worried that Marta had taken me for a total fool and wanted nothing to do with me. That was not at all in her nature, but you know how it is when your mind begins to get wrapped up in an idea.

"I was nearly on the verge of showing up at her front door, when finally I heard from her. One morning, I was rushing to a lecture—I always seemed to be rushing in those first few years of teaching—and stopped into my little office to get a book or some notes. I found on the ground an envelope with my name on it. I recognized the writing immediately. Marta had slipped a letter under my door. I slotted the envelope into my bag and rushed to class.

"I thought of nothing else during my lecture. I was desperate to open it. I went straight home after class and sat down at my dining room table. I was baffled by what was inside. I was expecting a heartfelt note of some sort, and at first I was sure it was just that. There were several pages of her beautiful cursive handwriting. I have kept the letter. In fact, I can show it to you. But at a glance, I could see that these were not her words. The words were from the New Testament. That is, she had copied out several pages from the gospels. Strange for a Jew, no?

"I skimmed through the pages once and was taken aback. My first thought was that she had lost her mind. Namely, that she had become some sort of convert, or maybe a religious fanatic. After all, the things we had been discussing—the Order of Tabitha and Lazarus—had a deeply spiritual dimension. That made no sense to me, though. That was not Marta. She was a good Polish Jew, no different than I. She was proud of her religious heritage, but she was no zealot. Why would she be bringing this up? I read the passage again. Clearly, the scripture was related to the stories of redemption and resurrection I had encountered in Lodz."

"What was the passage?" asked Aaron.

"She had transcribed the last chapters of the gospel of Luke, beginning with the road to Emmaus. Do you know that story?"

Aaron shook his head.

"You know the story. Jesus is crucified on Good Friday, then three days later—a short three days, I might add; I've slept that long on a Manischewitz hangover—he rises from the dead. On Easter Sunday, the women find the empty tomb, and they go and tell the men, and the men don't believe them. Preachers love making jokes about that. Who can resist? Even when your wife tells you the fridge is empty, you go and check, right? Peter goes back to inspect the empty tomb, and he still doesn't understand what's going on—doesn't matter that Jesus has been telegraphing this thing for months.

"Later on that day, a disciple named Cleopas and his companion, probably his wife, are on the road from Jerusalem to Emmaus. They were followers of Jesus; they had spent all their time with him. As they walk along, they're mourning his death, and a man comes upon them and asks them what they're discussing. They're shocked that this man has not heard about the death of Jesus. They explain to him who Jesus was and all that, and again they lament his death. As it turns out, the man apparently has heard of Jesus, and knows all the scriptures, as well. Then this mystery man gives Cleopas and his companion a kick in the pants. He tells them how foolish they are for not understanding the plan ordained by God.

"When they get to Emmaus in the evening, Cleopas and his companion beg the man to stay with them for the night. You see, they have a sense that this man is special. They don't want him to leave. He has a certain aura about him, and his knowledge of the scriptures is top notch. The man agrees to stay. They go into the house and sit down at the table, and the man prays over the meal. Suddenly—finally—Cleopas and his companion realize who this man is."

"Who is he?"

"The man is Jesus himself, raised from the dead!"

"The man who had been walking with them was Jesus?"

"Yes!" said Grandpa Moshe. "They hadn't recognized him the whole time, even though they were his followers! They had spent all their time with him, and still, they hadn't seen it!"

"But what does it mean?" asked Aaron.

"That's a very good question. I didn't have any clue what it meant."

"Then what did you do?"

"I'm afraid we must stop there," said Grandpa Moshe. "We're almost there."

Chapter Twenty-One

He Spoke

Aaron had been so absorbed in the story that he hadn't noticed where they were. Grandpa Moshe had pulled off the highway onto a rural road, heading away from the falling sun.

"Where are we?" asked Aaron.

"About an hour from home."

"Are we getting food?"

"No."

"Are we going home?"

"Not yet."

"Where are we going?"

"You'll see," said Grandpa Moshe.

Aaron shrank in his seat. Barely another car was on the road, and not a building in sight. All that Grandpa Moshe had told him was beginning to take hold of his imagination. He was worried he was caught up in something much bigger than he had realized, and somehow sinister.

"Why don't you want Professor Freeman to know about this?" asked Aaron.

"This information is sacred, Aaron. Not everyone is born into this. Michael is not yet a serious man. He means well, but he must bide his time."

"But then why did you tell him so much?"

Grandpa Moshe didn't respond. Aaron watched him.

"Grandpa?"

"I can't tell you exactly," said Grandpa Moshe. "There are times in life when you must stay the course, no matter what happens. You resist every possible obstacle or interference. And there are times when you must allow the river to steer the boat."

"What do you mean?"

"Somehow your professor has managed to put himself in a position to know about Lazarus. Over many, many years he has followed the trail. I know I am not the one to reveal the whole story of Lazarus to him, but I know I would be doing an immoral thing not to lead him further along the trail."

"I see," said Aaron. "I do think he means well."

"We all must suffer in uncertainty, but glimpses of knowledge—glimpses of a truth bigger than all of us and all of our silly ideas—that's what gives us hope, what gives us life."

For several minutes, they drove in silence along the winding, country roads as darkness fell on the hillsides and farm fields, dulling the glow of the setting sun.

"Do you remember the parable?" said Grandpa Moshe. "Have you figured it out?"

"Not really," said Aaron. "The only thing I have put together is that things are not what they seem. The prince is somehow not a prince, and the moat is somehow not a moat."

"That's very good. Things are not what they seem. Of course, there is more to the parables than just the endings. They are about seeking truth. I believe Michael may eventually learn the full truth about Lazarus, but it takes more than solving a riddle. He must not only understand the many lessons of the parables; he must live out the many lessons of the parables."

"But what do the parables mean?" asked Aaron. "What are the lessons?"

"That is the work of another day," said Grandpa Moshe. "That is the work of a lifetime. Now we have other things to learn."

Grandpa Moshe turned down an unmarked gravel lane. They listened to the crackling of rocks beneath the tires. The lane wound through a forest, and the country road behind them was soon obscured. An ominous wall of trees surrounded them. After a mile, the gravel lane began to climb up a gentle incline. When they reached the crest of the hill, a small valley opened before them. Down below, beyond the trees, was a sprawling mansion. They descended the other side of the hill, and the mansion disappeared behind the forest.

After another mile, the lights from the mansion shone through the trees. They emerged from the woods onto a grand drive lined with towering oaks. Beyond soaring ionic columns, sparkling light from chandeliers was visible through the enormous windows on the first floor. Grandpa Moshe inched along the looping stone path, skirting around the mansion. Passing the façade, Aaron saw the rest of the compound. Behind the mansion, a tiered garden extended into the night. Off to one side was a pool, glowing with underwater light, beside a pool house villa. Set off on a nearby rise was another huge house, in a complementary style.

"This isn't even the half of it," said Grandpa Moshe. "More houses are in the woods."

"Whose house is this?"

"Someone kind enough to host. Have you ever wondered where those billionaires you hear about live?"

"Yeah."

"This is it."

"Have you been here before?"

"Many years ago."

"There's no gate?"

"They've been watching us for at least a mile."

Grandpa Moshe parked the car and turned off the engine. He looked long at his grandson. Aaron waited.

"I don't need to tell you this," said Grandpa Moshe. "But I will. You know nothing about this place; you know nothing about the people in this room; you know nothing about what you are going to see and hear this evening."

Aaron felt feverish as they stepped out into the crisp air. He was lightheaded, nearly floating. Grandpa Moshe led the way across the property, toward a subterranean door tucked away on the side of the mansion. As they approached, an expressionless older man in a tailored black suit opened the door and stood aside. Grandpa Moshe nodded at the man as they went through the door. The man closed the door behind them.

They were clearly on a lower floor of the building, and yet the space was grand. The bright, coffered ceilings, high above them, were inlaid with intricate floral designs. The floors were marble, and on the walls were paintings and sketches, some of which Aaron was certain he recognized. The hallway was a veritable art gallery. Aaron drifted along in awe, his eyes shifting from one wall to the other, from painting to painting.

At the end of the hallway, they arrived at two heavy, dark wood doors with carved panels. One of the doors was slightly ajar. Grandpa Moshe stopped outside of the room, placing his palm on the closed door above one of the cast iron rings.

"These are the genuine article," said Grandpa Moshe. "Twelfth century, from a small chapel outside of Amiens. Most of the church was destroyed in the war. The rest of it is here."

Grandpa Moshe pushed open the door. Aaron stepped into the dim space, and immediately his eyes were drawn upward. Dark timber, a thousand years old, rose to the peak of the vaulted ceiling. The walls of the space were made of the original stone, complete with small, arched stained glass windows, backlit. The parts of the wall destroyed in the war were patched with smooth concrete, and broken stained glass had been replaced with panes of vermillion glass. Likewise, places where the ceiling had been repaired were made obvious by new timber, lighter in color. They had reconstructed a full chapel in the basement of the mansion.

Aaron felt a hand on his arm, awakening him from his spell. Grandpa Moshe nodded toward the pews. Several men and women were already sitting quietly, facing forward. Grandpa Moshe and Aaron slipped into an empty pew, and slid all the way down to one end. They waited. After a moment, the door opened, and Aaron instinctively checked over his shoulder. Grandpa Moshe patted him on the thigh. He subtly shook his head and pointed his finger forward.

"You know nothing about the people in this room," he whispered.

The pews gradually filled. Facing directly forward, Aaron examined the room as best he could. His roving eyes worked their way over the walls and ceiling, greedily absorbing the surfaces. Now and then, he noticed others filling the pews. All were discrete. They exuded nobility in their careful movements. There were no nods or subtle acknowledgements. Their decorum radiated across the sacred space, hazy and otherworldly in the glow of the stained glass.

The chapel, already silent, became more still when all the pews were filled. A door on the side of the small choir opened inward. A current of complete tranquility swept into the room, as if everyone had exhaled in unison. In the shadow of the doorway, a bent figure appeared. Aaron's heart fluttered and his hands began to tremble. The rush of adrenaline tingled in his limbs. He was delirious. He blinked in the faint light, struggling to comprehend what he was seeing.

The figure stepped forward from the doorway, straightening up. He was dressed in a black robe or tunic made of a coarse material, seemingly as old as the timbers and stones of the chapel. His long grey beard and full head of white hair were impressive and wild, without being unkempt. He was physically small, and yet somehow colossal—a giant. His presence was overwhelming. When he stood squarely in front of the church, a tidal wave of astonishment and reverence rolled over the pews. He sat, and the people in the pews breathed again.

"Good evening," said the old man.

The words hung in the air, reverberating through space. His voice was worn, somewhat high-pitched, without expressing even a hint of frailty. Instead, the voice was one of total authority. At the same time, his confidence gave him an air of casual familiarity. He spoke as though he knew every man and woman in the room, as if he was a close friend of each. Aaron was certain he recognized the man. Through all he had heard from Professor Freeman and his grandfather, he knew the man's eyes and voice. But there was something more, something beyond anything he had imagined. He was at once a superman, a demigod, and also his childhood friend, his most intimate acquaintance. This man, this Lazarus, was the universal man.

He spoke.

Chapter Twenty-Two

Marta's Secret

Lazarus said his last word.

Awe filled the chapel, each person spellbound. No one dared move. To applaud—to show any customary show of praise or approval—seemed out of place. No response could be commensurate. They had witnessed something of another world. They had seen the burning bush. The man in front of them existed in a different universe.

He was a specter, and he disappeared, as an apparition. Nodding at the people in the pews, Lazarus stood from his chair. He left through the door at the side of the small chapel choir.

The words of Professor Freeman came back to Aaron. What the man had said—all that the man claimed to be—could not be true according to any accepted measure of rational truth. The man was immortal. The man was Lazarus, born in the first century. The idea alone, apart from all the stories, was more than absurd. It was impossible. But the man could not be doubted, not even for a moment. He was more than human. He defied human laws. The idea that he did not exist—that he was not Lazarus—was impossible!

For several minutes, not a single person stirred. They remained where they were, not out of a sense of propriety, but because they were meditating on what they had heard. At last, one person left, and then another. Soon Grandpa Moshe patted Aaron on the thigh and nodded for them to leave. They walked out, through the medieval wood doors, down the august hallway. They followed the long gravel driveway through the dark woods and out onto the country road. Driving along the winding rural road back to the highway, they remained mesmerized.

At last, as they neared the house, Grandpa Moshe put his hand on Aaron's forearm, awaking him from his reverie.

"Are you okay?" he asked. "What are you thinking?"

"I don't know," said Aaron. "I'm thinking about everything."

"About the stories?"

"About the stories, about the man—about everything."

"I understand. You look as I'm sure I looked after that evening in Lodz."

"I just can't wrap my mind around it," said Aaron.

Grandpa Moshe nodded. They went on in silence, following the familiar route back to the house. They pulled into the driveway, and Grandpa Moshe turned off the engine.

"Can you just tell me?" said Aaron.

"Can I just tell you?"

"Is it true?"

"Let me continue what I was telling you before," said Grandpa Moshe.

They turned the lights on in the dark house. Grandpa Moshe immediately went to the living room and collapsed in his favorite armchair. Aaron went to the kitchen and returned with a glass of water for his grandfather, who pressed his eyes closed and took a long sip. He was sunken in his chair, exhausted.

"Have you thought any more about the parables?" asked Grandpa Moshe.

Aaron hesitated, surprised by the question.

"It's okay," said Grandpa Moshe. "Let me go on. As I was saying, my mentor had given me this passage about Jesus and Cleopas on the road to Emmaus, written out in beautiful, flawless handwriting. I knew that this information was vitally important; I just didn't know what my mentor was trying to tell me. Everything was tied together somehow, but I couldn't solve the riddle. I reviewed what I had told Marta, about my meeting with Agata and about the Order of Tabitha. I wondered if the Bible passage was meant as some sort of analogy relating to Agata's change of identity. I reviewed all the stories Lazarus had told us, and I considered this man who had called himself Lazarus. I racked my brain for hours before deciding I simply had to find Marta and ask her bluntly what it all meant.

"That afternoon, I went to Marta's office. She wasn't there—I hadn't found her there in days. I happened to see one of her colleagues in a nearby office, however. I asked him if she was around. Marta was in Europe, he told me. She was giving a lecture in West Germany. I smiled and nodded, as casually as I could, but I was annoyed. Why hadn't she told me she was leaving? At that point, in a way, I was almost more concerned about Marta and our friendship than about the mystery I was trying to solve. I had shared very sensitive information with her, and she was behaving strangely."

"What did you do?" asked Aaron.

"I could do nothing until she came back," said Grandpa Moshe. "There was no Internet at that point. I couldn't call her cell phone or send her an email. Even if I could have, I wouldn't have. The only way to talk about the whole thing was to speak in person. I had no choice but to wait. I barely slept. I could think of nothing else. I became neurotic. I would swing back and forth. One moment, I convinced myself of the most outlandish theories, and the next moment I dismissed the whole situation as being a figment of my imagination, a reaction to my dramatic encounter with Agata.

"The next week, Marta returned from her trip to West Germany. When I stopped by her office, she was out of sorts. Her cheeks were flush. She was standing over her desk, rifling through papers. I could see she was in the process of catching up on all her tasks. As soon as she saw me in the doorway, she breathed a sigh of relief and collapsed into her chair. I asked her some friendly questions about her trip, but I could not resist for long. I closed her door.

"I said, 'Marta, I received your note. You must tell me what all this means.'

"She smiled mischievously, and she had a twinkle in her eye.

" 'I am going mad!' I begged. 'I can't think about anything else!'

" 'Oh, Moshe,' she said, 'you still do not see.'

"I shook my head.

" 'Look at me,' she said. 'Look me in the eyes. You still don't see?'

"I stared at her, wondering what on earth I could be missing. I couldn't tell which one of us was crazier.

"Finally, she slid open one of her desk drawers and brought out a Hebrew prayer book. She beckoned me to come closer. I leaned forward in my chair, across the desk. In a whisper, she began to read a blessing. My heart nearly stopped. My hair stood up on my arms. Still, I didn't quite know what I was hearing. Her voice was strange—not her own voice. Then it struck me. I literally fell out of my chair—I fell on one knee. I was in complete shock. I stood up, knocking over my chair. Marta leaned back in her chair with a coy smile."

The front door suddenly opened, startling Aaron.

"Hello?" called a voice.

"Miriam," said Grandpa Moshe. "We're in here."

"We?" she called back.

After a long moment, Aaron's mother appeared in the doorway to the living room. Seeing Aaron, she put her hands on her hips and cocked her head.

"What are you doing here?"

"Grandpa picked me up at school," said Aaron.

Miriam's brow clouded. She glared at Grandpa Moshe.

"Where have you been?" she demanded.

"Miriam," said Grandpa Moshe, "you know where we've been."

Aaron's mother sighed and shook her head. She sat down on the couch in the living room, across from Aaron and Grandpa Moshe.

"The old Lazarus hoax," she said. "It just won't die, will it?"

Grandpa Moshe sat back in his chair and crossed his arms. She sat forward on the couch, turning to Aaron.

"What did he say?" she said. "What did spooky Mr. Lazarus tell you?"

Aaron hesitated, glancing at his grandfather.

"Well," she said. "What did he say? Don't think I haven't heard all these stories before."

Aaron said nothing.

"Really, tell me," pressed his mother more sincerely.

"I can't," said Aaron. "I mean, how could I? I can't do it. I can't reproduce it."

"Tell me. Tell me what he said. Tell me what you remember. I'm serious. I'm curious."

Aaron dropped his head and rubbed the back of his neck. Grandpa Moshe patted Aaron on the knee.

"Go on, Aaron," said Grandpa Moshe. "Tell the story of the legionnaire. That was one of the shorter stories. Begin with Julius Caesar."

Aaron shook his head helplessly.

"Go on, Aaron. You remember it."

"The first story," said Aaron, "the first thing he told us, was about Julius Caesar."

Miriam nodded at her son and raised her eyebrows. She sat up straight on the sofa with her hands folded.

Chapter Twenty-Three

The Roman Legionnaire

"Julius Caesar was a man of many faults," Aaron began. "He was a cruel man. He was a vicious man. He was a man of massacres. Men, women, children. His own soldiers. Murder, to him, was nothing. He did not have an appetite for death, no more than one has an appetite for breathing. He simply killed whenever necessary—without thought, without compunction. He was not immoral. He was above morals. He was above men. He was a tyrant god."

Aaron stopped. He glanced from his mother to his grandfather.

"Very good," said Grandpa Moshe. "That's just as I remember it."

Aaron shrugged and started again.

"But, ironically, despite his incredible cruelty, Julius Caesar was not a bad emperor for the Jews, who had had a precarious, if not entirely perilous existence under Roman rule. His reign instituted one of the greatest periods of security for the Jews of the era, for it was Julius Caesar who officially recognized Judaism as a legal religion. The accommodating treatment of the Jews continued under Emperor Augustus. In fact, during the first decades of his reign, the Jews established the Jewish quarter of Rome, which exists to this day on the banks of the Tiber.

"But sadly, as the Jews have always found in the course of their long history of survival, the peace was not to last. In the first century, tensions began to increase in the Roman province of Judea, and when the Roman Empire came on hard times, the tensions boiled over. Under Caligula—the emperor known maybe more than any other emperor for his cruelty—the relationship between the Romans and the Jews deteriorated rapidly, turning into an open conflict almost over night. The strife went on for decades, leading up to the event that remains fixed in the collective memory of the Jews. Under the emperor Titus, in the year 70, I believe . . ."

"That's right," said Grandpa Moshe.

"The Romans destroyed the temple."

Aaron's mother nodded. She had settled comfortably into the sofa with her arms crossed.

"That famous moment in time when the Romans seized Jerusalem and massacred the Jews was thoroughly documented by the era's historians. In the spring of that year, the emperor Titus surrounded the city of Jerusalem with his legions, preparing for an attack just three days before the Passover celebration. The city was swarming with Jewish pilgrims, who would be trapped along with the rebels and other inhabitants in the captured city. Over the course of four months, hundreds of thousands of Jews perished, many of them innocent pilgrims from distant lands.

"What was not as well documented by historians of the time, and what can never be fully documented in any war, are the heroic tales of survival. As the temple burned, and the Roman soldiers slaughtered anyone in sight—it was a Roman custom to massacre and enslave—the Jews fled in every direction, including through the extensive underground networks. Some of them scurried into the sewer system, and others escaped through tunnels built by the rebels.

"The city was utter chaos—a scene of bloodshed and mayhem of biblical proportions. The methodical, strategic plan to take the city had devolved into a maelstrom of savage murder. In most cases, the Roman soldiers were too distracted by the orgy of death and destruction to pursue all the fleeing rebels and bystanders. They were simply killing opportunistically, lashing out with their swords and spears at anyone who came near. Their only objective was to massacre. They transformed the city into a cesspool of terror.

"Now, as I said, or as Lazarus said, the massacre was in many ways disorganized, which allowed the escape and survival of fighters and innocent people alike. But, as in any battle through the ages that explodes into chaos and unbridled killing, there were those who were bent on horrifying acts of carnage—those who lost their minds, who became instruments of the Devil himself.

"Among the many legions, there was a lone centurion who, even in the midst of total disorder, quickly became a marked man for his evil deeds. He was not only indiscriminate in his slaughter of men, women and children; he was also gruesome in a way that appalled even the other Roman soldiers. He had left humanity behind. He was a beast. The soldiers in his own cohort began to fear him. Some did all they could to avoid him, while others followed him in quiet dread. Still others became his passionate disciples, mesmerized by his wickedness. With this man as their leader, they formed a unit of murderers, a merciless death squad.

"Every day and into the night, these men thirsted for blood. They went on homicidal binges, searching out victims door to door, putting their own lives at risk in their quest for more bloodshed. They reported to no one, ignoring the warnings of the other centurions and the directives of the commander of the legion. Their only purpose was to kill as many of the people of Jerusalem as they could find, and they took special satisfaction in finding rebels and other innocent people who thought they had escaped the massacre. They relished the discovery of a secret refuge or hidden tunnel.

"During one of their many terrorizing forays through Jerusalem, one among this group of legionnaires, led by their mad centurion, happened upon a strange sight. They were marauding through the streets, returning to their encampment, when this soldier happened to glance down a narrow street between buildings. A gleam in the darkness had caught his eye. He stopped to look more closely, and saw a cluster of small, shining disks in the distance. Forgetting the other soldiers, the legionnaire stepped deeper into the alley, squinting in the darkness. As he got closer, he realized what he was seeing. A group of small children were squeezed against a wall at the end of the alley, huddled together like cats.

"So possessed was this legionnaire by the spirit of evil, that he smiled at his discovery, as though the Devil had presented these indefensible children for slaughter. His greed for blood was so great that he did not even go to tell the other soldiers of what he had found. He planned to take all the bloodshed for himself. He sneered with delight, and the little children squeezed closer together, trembling in terror. As he approached, he brought out his sword from its sheath and raised it above his head.

"But before he could come upon the children, he felt the touch of a hand on his raised forearm. He jumped back, prepared to strike out with his sword. He was confused by what he saw. A dark figure with glowing eyes, dressed in a black cloak with a hood, had emerged from the shadows. The legionnaire immediately sensed that the man before him was a man of authority. The shadowy figure removed his hood, revealing his white hair. His eyes became sharper. The legionnaire trembled.

" 'What do you want with me?' shouted the legionnaire.

"The old man said nothing. He stepped closer to the legionnaire, and the legionnaire backed up, his sword raised. For some unknown reason, he could not strike him. Yet he remained poised to defend himself against the strange power of the old man. The legionnaire retreated until he bumped into the wall behind him. He was huffing in terror, hyperventilating, as the old man came closer, until they were face to face in the alleyway. They stared into each other's eyes. The legionnaire could not bear the burning gaze of the old man.

" 'Get away!' he shouted. 'Leave me!'

"The old man slowly raised his arm. He laid his hand on the legionnaire's hand, which tightly gripped the sword. The mere touch of the old man's hand caused the weapon to fall. The old man held the legionnaire's hand and turned it over, so that the palm was open. As he did so, the legionnaire could feel a change coming over him, a feeling of liberation, as if the demon that had possessed him was fleeing.

" 'These children do not need the sword,' said the old man. 'The sword has left them orphaned and starving. They need food. Now go.'

"The legionnaire looked down once more at the huddled children. Seeing their eyes, he suddenly recognized the full extent of his wickedness. Only a moment before, he had been prepared to butcher them. Tears flooded his eyes. The legionnaire fell to his knees, begging forgiveness. He scrambled away down the dark alley, back out into the streets.

"When the legionnaire returned to the encampment, in the occupied area of the city, he found the evil centurion and his band reveling by the fire, slopping up food and drink. The legionnaire snuck around them, avoiding being seen. Finding the foodstuffs, he filled a large satchel with as much as he could fit. He also took a blanket and snuck back out into the night. Risking his life, as a lone foreign soldier in an enemy city, he went to the alley where he had seen the small children. He kneeled before them and laid the satchel of food at their feet and spread the blanket over them. He snuck away through the city, back to the encampment.

"The next day, the soldier went into battle with his legion, but stayed in line with his cohort, and did not stray into the wild bouts of bloodletting that inevitably arose. He stayed as far as he could from the mad centurion and his followers. Once night had fallen on the day of combat, and the Romans had returned to the occupied area, the legionnaire waited for quiet in the camp. He again gathered what he could, even picking up scraps of discarded food, and went back to the alley. Day after day, he left the Roman army without permission, putting his life on the line, to feed these orphans of the war.

"One night, after two weeks of nurturing the needy children whenever he could, the legionnaire returned to the dark, narrow street to find that the children were gone. Immediately, he feared the worst, that the children had been put to the sword, or had simply fallen prey to starvation, or any of the other perils of the war-torn city. But once more, Lazarus appeared from the shadows. He placed his hand on the legionnaire's cheek.

" 'The children are safe,' he told him. 'God has seen your goodness. Go.'

"The legionnaire was brought to tears. He returned to the Roman camp a new man. Maintaining his loyalty to the Roman Empire, he stayed in his post and did all he could to salvage humanity. He pressed his comrades to be merciful and just. In a matter of months, Jerusalem was sacked, but the war between the Romans and the Jews continued. The Jewish rebels fled Jerusalem, defending strongholds at Herodium and Machaerus and Masada, before finally succumbing. When the fighting had ceased, the legionnaire at last abandoned his post. Forsaking the rewards for his service to the Roman Empire, he returned to Jerusalem to help the Jewish people rebuild their city."

Aaron faltered slightly as he finished. He had been in a trance as he recalled every detail of the story as best he could. His grandfather's voice woke him from his stupor.

"That's not bad, Aaron," said Grandpa Moshe. "Not at all bad."

"Yes, not bad," said his mother. "A little bit stiff in parts—a little bit academic, maybe—but yes, quite good, Aaron."

Aaron stared at his mother, and then at his grandfather, baffled by their reaction.

"I don't understand," said Aaron.

Chapter Twenty-Four

Elijah's Passover Cloak

Miriam squeezed Aaron's knee, and smiled maternally, almost winking.

"I don't get it," persisted Aaron. "Is this some kind of test?"

"That's a good start," she said.

Miriam spoke in a tone Aaron had rarely seen. So often she was jocular or neurotic, almost theatrical. Sometimes she played her role as an anxious mother and a fretting professor as an act, an adopted persona. Now she reached out and took Aaron by the hand. She pressed his hand, and smiled warmly, her eyes glassed over with tears.

"In fact," said Miriam, "that is very good. You have a lot of promise."

"I don't understand," repeated Aaron.

"Aaron," she said, "do you remember when you were a small child, the first year we moved into this house, and the first year Grandpa Moshe came to live with us?"

Aaron nodded.

"Do you remember on Passover; we asked you and the other little children to go to the door at the end of the meal to check for the prophet Elijah? Do you remember what happened?"

Aaron turned to Grandpa Moshe, who nodded with a grin.

"Do you?" said Miriam.

"Of course," said Aaron. "The other kids and I went to the door. We were a little bit spooked, as usual. But I was the oldest, I think, so I pretended I wasn't afraid or anything. I opened the door wide, as wide as it would go. We were all standing in the doorway when Grandpa Moshe jumped out in a black cloak and screamed."

"That's right," his mother said with a laugh. "Now I'm going to ask you again, just as when you were a child, to go check the door."

Aaron's brow wrinkled in confusion, turning from his mother to his grandfather. Grandpa Moshe waved him toward the door.

"What?" said Aaron. "What is going on?"

"Go check the door," said Miriam.

Aaron stood up from the couch. His hands were trembling. His mother and grandfather sat patiently, showing no signs of mockery or playfulness. Once more, as he had many times over the previous few weeks, Aaron had the sensation that he was dreaming. He could not make sense of what was happening. As if in a film, he had stumbled upon a massive conspiracy, some strange and sinister plot. But this wasn't a film. And there was nothing nefarious about what was happening. And the actors were his own family members—his own mother and grandfather!

Aaron drifted out of the living room, into the front hall, which was dimly lit by the light from the living room. He hesitated, like a child awake in the night, frightened to go out into the hallway. Standing in the wide doorway to the front hall, he felt along the wall and flicked on the overhead light. At first, he saw nothing unusual. He cautiously moved toward the door, and something caught his eye. A chill ran through him. Next to the front door, hanging on a hook, was a coarse black cloak.

Aaron recognized the material immediately. In a daze, he got the cloak down from the hook. The cloth hung heavily from his hand. He flopped the garment over his arm and felt the texture between his thumb and finger. He stood frozen, staring at the cloak.

"Aaron," called Grandpa Moshe.

Aaron said nothing. He was at a loss. Incoherent thoughts ran through his head. His mother and grandfather appeared in the doorway of the front hall. They watched him. He looked up at them and shook his head in disbelief.

"Aaron," said his mother. "Come sit down."

Aaron sat on the couch in a stupor, the robe of Lazarus draped across his lap. He rested his open hands on the cloth, as if holding a talisman. For a moment, Miriam and Grandpa Moshe watched him, waiting for him to speak. But he said nothing.

"I know this has been a lot to take in," said Grandpa Moshe. "The truth is that we had no intention of telling you all this—not yet."

"We were waiting for the right time," said Miriam. "We were waiting until you were a bit older—until you were at least out of college—but we felt we couldn't wait any longer. We had no idea that your professor knew of Lazarus, and we had no idea that he would tell you. Those who have seen Lazarus are sworn to secrecy."

"I hope that old fool hasn't been telling every undergraduate who wants to listen," mumbled Grandpa Moshe.

"I still don't understand," said Aaron. "Who is Lazarus? Who is Marta?"

Miriam deferred to her father. Grandpa Moshe shifted his weight in his armchair.

"Let me finish what I was saying," he said. "All will be explained."

Chapter Twenty-Five

The Voice Behind the Veil

Grandpa Moshe sighed and got to his feet and stood before Aaron.

"Before your mother walked in," he began, "I was telling you about my mentor, about the moment when she read that prayer to me. The voice was not hers, Aaron. It was the voice of the haunting old man I had heard speak in Lodz."

Grandpa Moshe placed his hands on Aaron's shoulders.

"Aaron," he said. "It was the voice of Lazarus."

Aaron nodded, spellbound. Grandpa Moshe shuffled back to his seat.

"And suddenly everything made sense," he continued. "I was Cleopas. The whole time, I had been walking the road to Emmaus with my mentor, my teacher, not realizing that she was Lazarus.

"Now, I'm sure you'll understand the two parables. Of course, at the time, I only knew the one parable about the prince. But immediately it made perfect sense. Remember what you said earlier, Aaron. Remember the parables. Things are not as they seem. The moat was not a moat. The moat was quicksand. The prince was not a prince."

"The prince was a princess."

"Yes," said Grandpa Moshe. "The prince was a princess."

"But the parable is a trick," said Aaron. "They saw the prince!"

"No, no, no. You are forgetting. No one outside of the palace had ever seen the prince face to face. Only the one woman saw her from a distance, behind a veil."

"Behind a veil."

"That's right. She was behind a veil."

"In disguise."

"Exactly. Marta had a perfect disguise. So perfect that even I couldn't see that my mentor was Lazarus. That's the whole point! As long as she was not Lazarus, no one was Lazarus. And if no one was Lazarus, then Lazarus was real.

"There was no way for me to know, even though I saw her every day. If I, who spent hour after hour with her, could not see that she was Lazarus, how could anyone ever see that she was Lazarus? No one could see beyond the veil, and her intellect was unassailable. You couldn't stump her. Her mind was too brilliant, and she told only the truth. The only lie was the existence of Lazarus."

"But then . . ."

Aaron paused, not knowing how to go on. He stared at the ground, shaking his head. The truth was impossible.

"Yes?" said Grandpa Moshe.

"I don't understand. Who is Lazarus?"

"Ah," said Grandpa Moshe. "You, too, are like Cleopas. You, too, have not seen."

Aaron's mother abruptly stood up from the couch.

"We want to show you something," she said. "Bring the robe."

Aaron followed his mother back out into the front hall, past the staircase, around to the basement door. She turned on the light and stood on the top stair.

"Do you remember, Aaron, when we first bought this house? You were just a child then."

"I remember," said Aaron.

"Do you remember we had to wait a year before we moved in?"

"Yeah, when they were doing construction. We used to come visit the house, when we were still at the apartment in Cambridge. We would drive out here and have a picnic on the floor in the living room. There was no furniture."

"That's right," said Miriam. "Now I will show you what they were working on."

She started down the stairs to the basement, Aaron and Grandpa Moshe in tow. Straight ahead at the bottom of the stairs was a laundry room. To one side was space for the water heater and other utilities. To the other side of the staircase was a small room with a warped old ping-pong table, crammed in next to storage shelves. A single light bulb hung from the ceiling. The basement space was small—too small for a house that large, it suddenly occurred to Aaron.

His mother walked into the laundry room and pulled the string on the light bulb.

"You haven't spent much time in this room, have you?"

"I guess not," laughed Aaron.

"And you've spent no time in the room I'm about to show you."

Miriam stood directly in front of the laundry machine as Aaron looked over her shoulder. The tall machine, a stacked washer and drier, reached from floor to ceiling. She kicked out a metal lock on one side and pushed the machine, which glided easily across the concrete floor on a concealed track. Behind the laundry machine appeared to be a concrete wall, the same as all the other concrete walls in the basement, with regular seams every few feet, showing where the concrete was molded.

Miriam stepped into the space vacated by the laundry machine. She undid a disguised latch near the floor, and another near the ceiling. Pressing against the wall with her fingertips, a door opened between two of the seams in the concrete foundation.

"This cannot be real," said Aaron.

"Just wait," said Grandpa Moshe.

"Watch your step," said Miriam.

She passed through the dark opening, down two steps. As soon as she entered the space, fluorescent lights automatically flickered on. The room was at least half the size of the first floor of the house, perhaps larger, and the ceilings were higher than the rest of the house. Rows of tall, modern shelves, made of plastic and metal, filled the room. Aaron stared in awe, the black robe still hanging from his arm.

"I'll take that," said Miriam.

She hung up the robe on a hook. As they walked into the room, the electric buzz of the shelves caused Aaron's ears to perk up. Miriam put her hand on one of the shelves.

"The same kind we have on campus," she said.

She pressed a button, and one of the shelves shifted slowly on a mechanical track, providing access to a new aisle of books. Aaron examined the shelves, mesmerized by the collection of books and documents. He reached up to touch one of the bindings.

"Be careful," said Grandpa Moshe. "Some of these are quite old—centuries old."

Aaron ran his finger along a row of books, without touching them. They were all clearly works of historical interest, although many were unmarked. At a glance, he saw firsthand accounts and journals and registers. Most of the books appeared to be old and rare, but some were more recent works of history.

"Where did these all come from?" asked Aaron.

"They've been collected over millennia," said Grandpa Moshe.

Aaron saw beyond Grandpa Moshe, to the other side of the room. There was a carpeted reading space with comfortable chairs and lamps, and two large desks with computers. Documents and notes were neatly spread out across the desks.

"Come over here," said Miriam. "I have something else to show you."

Aaron followed his mother to the far end of the space, past the reading area and the shelves, to a back wall covered by a heavy black curtain. Miriam pulled the curtain cords, hand over hand. The black velvet separated and bunched, revealing an extensive glass bookcase, completely sealed. Miriam turned a dial, flooding the display case with a soft, foggy light.

"These are the most delicate, and the oldest," she said.

Aaron leaned forward, peering through the glass at the collection of ancient books and records. Before him were the works of a museum. He pored over the frayed pages of illuminated manuscripts, complete with decorative letters and margin illustrations. The shelves contained books with wooden covers, scrolls and worn leather journals, tattered pages from letters.

As Aaron scanned the panoply of historical records, his mother handed him a pair of soft white gloves. She opened one of the glass windows with a key and delicately removed a slim, unmarked volume, bound in thin wood and leather. She went to the nearby desk, and Aaron followed. She let him hold the object, which was nearly weightless in his hands, before setting the book down on the desk.

"Papyrus," she said.

Bending her head over the desk, she carefully separated the cover from the first page. The writing was nearly impossible to read, but he recognized the letters as Hebrew.

"Can you guess what it is?" she asked.

Aaron shook his head. Miriam pointed out a jumble of letters partway down the tattered page. Aaron bent over, scrutinizing the page. He could decipher some of the letters.

"Roman?"

"That's right," she said. "This is the account of the Roman legionnaire."

"Why is it in Hebrew?"

"The story continues from where you left off. The legionnaire, as you said, went back to Jerusalem to help the city rebuild after the war. He offered all he could as an illiterate soldier, and was eventually adopted, in a sense, by an order of scribes, who taught him to read and write in Hebrew and Latin. This account details much more than just the events of the Roman siege of Jerusalem. After many years in Jerusalem, the legionnaire returned to Rome as an ambassador, a mediator. He went back and forth for years, striving to bring peace. Of course, the Romans and the Jews were in conflict throughout his life."

"He produced this account in both Hebrew and Latin," added Grandpa Moshe. "But only the Hebrew survived."

"Let me read from the first page," said Miriam. "Sit down."

Grandpa Moshe gently pushed Aaron toward one of the comfortable armchairs. Miriam coughed, clearing her throat, and gently picked up the ancient manuscript.

She spoke.

And the voice was not hers. Aaron staggered backwards, overcome, and fell into the armchair. Tears brimmed in his eyes. He heard the voice he had heard that very evening, delivered through the veil of a long gray beard and a black cloak. He heard the voice of Lazarus.

"Mom?"

Miriam looked Aaron in the eyes. She nodded.

Chapter Twenty-Six

A Library Millennia in the Making

Aaron was in shock. Grandpa Moshe placed his hand on his shoulder to steady him in his armchair. They all sat down in the carpeted space. Aaron swallowed, incapable of words, his eyes wide. Grandpa Moshe and Miriam gave him time.

"How could this be?" he said at last. "It's impossible. This whole time."

Miriam smiled, nodding.

"Mom, are you a genius?"

"I thought you'd never ask!"

Miriam and Grandpa Moshe enjoyed the joke, but Aaron was too bewildered to laugh.

"You might be surprised what many years of careful study can produce," said Grandpa Moshe. "You should try it some time."

"I have so many questions," Aaron interrupted earnestly. "How long has this been going on? I don't understand. My whole life?"

"Oh, much longer than that," said Grandpa Moshe. "Longer than your mother's life, longer than my life. This has been going on for centuries, Aaron."

"We built this library during the first year we owned the property," said Miriam. "Of course, the construction was only one part of the project. We spent months and months smuggling these materials into the house. Many books we could simply load up in vans, or even ship. But other manuscripts required the utmost care, as you can see."

"Where do they all come from?" asked Aaron.

"All over. Lazarus is two thousand years old, but this library—this collection—is new. This is the first of its kind. This library was scattered across the globe. We have assembled papers from Europe, and the Middle East, from North Africa and South America, and even from this country."

"How did you find them all? How did you get them?"

"This is the first complete collection," said Grandpa Moshe. "But it is not the first collection. I'm sure you will remember a small detail from the stories I told you, Aaron, the stories from my search for Agata."

Aaron leaned back in his chair in thought, sifting through the long string of narratives from the past days and weeks.

"Remember the room in the house where I met Agata," said Grandpa Moshe. "Remember the front room in the mansion of Tabitha, the grand hall they transformed into a chapel."

"Of course!" said Aaron. "The books. The shelves."

"That's right," said Grandpa Moshe.

"How did you get them here?"

"Through a lot of patient work," said Miriam, "beginning long before you were born. After the Second World War, as Europe recovered, the last remaining members at the house in Belgium, the home of the Order of Tabitha, neared their death. The rapidly changing landscape left little room for the estate. Women were called into the world. They no longer appeared at the doors of the mansion in Flanders. What could they do? They arranged to have the library shipped to the United States. Already, at that point, the followers of Tabitha had determined that America would be the safest place for their collection. They began a project to transfer all these materials here, and to have them digitally copied.

"But the Order of Tabitha did not disappear when the last members died. Pockets of underground followers had already begun to spring up all over the world, including in Lodz, where they had been compiling their own library of rare books. Many years passed before we could safely transport the collection in Lodz, though. The risks were too great."

"The Berlin Wall," said Aaron.

"Exactly. Only a few years before you were born, we were finally able to begin transporting the collection of books from the house in Lodz."

"Transported where? I don't understand. This library wasn't here yet."

"A certain house in New Jersey," said Grandpa Moshe.

"Your house?"

"No, no, no," said Grandpa Moshe. "You're forgetting an important character."

"Of course," said Aaron. "Your mentor."

"Each time Marta went to Europe, or the Middle East, or to South America, she brought back books—books and manuscripts and letters—given to her by the followers of Tabitha."

"And Agata was one of them."

"Yes, Agata was one of them."

"Did you ever see her again?"

"I never saw her again. Twenty years ago, when the Eastern Bloc had opened, when you were just a child, I went on a mission to Poland to retrieve the rest of the books from the house in Lodz. By then, I had been happily married. Still, I was moved to tears. I stood outside on the street, where I had stood decades before, and remembered how I had felt. When I went to the house, an aged woman answered the door. Somehow, I knew immediately that Agata was no longer there. Few women were left in the house, and Agata was not among them. I said my final goodbyes to Agata there. I knelt on the stones outside the house and recited the Kaddish."

"What happened to the house?"

"The house is no more," said Grandpa Moshe. "The remaining women were not able to stay in the house for long—not in the changing world. The war, the Holocaust, had increased the flock. And the hardships of communism had kept many minds fixed on things of the spirit. But as comforts grew, fewer and fewer understood the meaning of an ascetic life."

"How did you get the books back?" asked Aaron.

"By that time, it was simple. The technology had changed. I didn't have to smuggle them out in my suitcases and coat pockets. I arranged to have all the items shipped, some of them by the most advanced methods. The most delicate items were handled by professionals, shipped using the same procedures used by the best museums in the world."

"That sounds expensive."

"The best methods are never cheap. They cost time or money, usually both."

"But how could you afford it?"

"You saw where we were earlier this evening," said Grandpa Moshe. "You saw that billionaire's compound. The network is not insignificant."

"This sounds like a classic conspiracy theory."

Miriam and Grandpa Moshe laughed.

"That's right," said Miriam. "Conspiracy theories come from somewhere."

Aaron shook his head in disbelief. He stood up and swung around, scanning the basement library that had always existed without his knowledge, beneath the floorboards. He had to remind himself he was standing in his childhood home. He was living in an alternate reality.

"It's getting late," said Grandpa Moshe. "We better go up. We can continue talking tomorrow. We still have much to discuss, much more than we can cover in a night."

Grandpa Moshe pushed himself up from his armchair with a grimace, creaking his back into an upright position. Miriam returned the manuscript of the legionnaire to the display case and locked the glass. She turned off the lights and pulled the heavy black curtains closed. Grandpa Moshe had made his way to the door. He watched Aaron, who remained frozen in the middle of the room, staring off in a daze.

"Is it all a hoax?" said Aaron. "Is it a game?"

"You can see that this is no hoax," said Grandpa Moshe. "The library is real. The Order of Tabitha is real. The network is real. This is not a game."

"But all the stories? What's true and what's not? Are the stories real?"

"You've seen them yourself," said Miriam. "They are all from these shelves."

"But still, are they true?"

"They could be," said Grandpa Moshe. "Not all historical accounts are verifiable. Some of them are simply impossible to verify. That doesn't mean they're not true."

Miriam had walked over to the door. She waited with Grandpa Moshe.

"Not one story is made up," she said. "Every story of Lazarus ever told comes from this library, or other libraries—from centuries of letters and books and accounts."

"What about Lazarus? Is he in the stories?"

Grandpa Moshe smiled. He bowed his head. Aaron turned to his mother. She also smiled. After a moment, she shook her head.

"In other words, Lazarus is just completely made up," said Aaron. "There is no Lazarus."

"Not exactly," said Miriam.

"But, I mean, the real Lazarus is dead."

"I don't know," said Grandpa Moshe. "I wouldn't say that."

"I get it—you keep him alive with the stories."

"No, not quite. There is more to it than that."

"What do you mean?"

"My mentor, Aaron."

"Your mentor?"

"Yes, my mentor, Marta. She was more than my mentor, Aaron."

"We should go back upstairs," said Miriam.

Chapter Twenty-Seven

A Society with No Name

Aaron followed his mother and grandfather out of the library. Miriam pulled the concrete door shut behind him. She latched the door at the top and bottom, and slid the laundry machine unit back across the floor and locked it in place with her foot.

"You don't need a key," she told Aaron. "This space is open to you. But do not open the glass cabinet without me."

Aaron nodded distantly. The three went back upstairs to the living room. Aaron collapsed onto the couch, brooding. He watched his grandfather. The fatigue of the day was wearing heavily on his shoulders. He shuffled across the living room, to a cabinet in the far corner, beyond the television, and opened a drawer. He brought out a picture frame. Bent, he gazed at the photograph. A faint smile appeared on his lips. He pulled his sleeve over his hand and wiped off the glass. He shuffled over to the couch and sat down next to Aaron.

"Have you seen this picture?" said Grandpa Moshe.

"Yeah," said Aaron.

"Do you know who it is?"

"That's you, right?"

Grandpa Moshe nodded. They examined the black and white photograph of a young family. A young girl was seated between her parents and her grandmother, her feet dangling from a park bench.

"And that's you, mom?"

Miriam nodded.

"That was only a couple years before we lost her," said Grandpa Moshe. "None of us knew it then, but your grandmother Deborah already had lung cancer at that time. That evil thing was already inside of her when we took that picture. We found out six months later. There was nothing we could do."

"And who is that?"

"That is your great grandmother, Aaron."

Miriam nodded. She put her hand on Aaron's shoulder.

"My grandmother," said Miriam, "Marta."

"What?" exclaimed Aaron. "Why haven't you ever told me this?"

"Oh, Aaron. We have told you many times about your great-grandmother. These things mean nothing to the young."

Aaron shook his head incredulously.

"Your great-grandmother did not mean anything to you," said Miriam, "until now."

"And that's okay," said Grandpa Moshe. "You must begin to have a past before you can begin to appreciate the past."

Aaron stared at his great-grandmother Marta. She was dressed in a skirt suit with a blouse. She had a short, elegant hairstyle.

"She looks like you," said Aaron.

"A little," agreed Miriam.

"You have seen her picture before," said Grandpa Moshe. "The picture Professor Freeman showed you was not just a picture of my old philosophy professor, but a picture of your great-grandmother—dressed in drag, as they say."

"Dressing in drag is a family tradition," laughed Miriam.

"How did this happen?" said Aaron.

"Much of it is very simple," explained Grandpa Moshe. "I fell in love."

Grandpa Moshe took the photograph out of Aaron's hands. He slowly rose to his feet and shuffled across the room to place the photograph on the mantelpiece.

The Rise of Lazarus

"My life changed when I found out that Marta was Lazarus. You can imagine! A good mentor will change your life, but she was now so much more. I knew that I had no choice but to follow her. I became more than a mentee; I became a disciple. Over time, Marta initiated me. She explained the intricate workings of this society of Lazarus. She instructed me on her role. More importantly, two years after my trip to Poland, Marta introduced me to her daughter Deborah, who had just finished her doctorate. I fell in love, for the second time.

"Deborah was destined to take on the mantle of Lazarus. She was to inherit the robe from her mother Marta, and I was to inherit the role of chief counsel. All our waking hours—all our hours outside of teaching—we devoted to learning the materials. We pored over the documents, and we began transcribing them. We read all the research ever written, from our time, and from centuries past. Marta was our instructor. She taught us the history, the stories she had learned over time. Nothing is more important than knowledge. Nothing is more important than the past.

"But tragedy struck. I have never known a stronger woman than Deborah. She was as brilliant as her mother, and as courageous. But she met an enemy she could not defeat. Within just a few quick years, cancer took her. For the second time, the love of my life was ripped from my arms."

"It makes no sense," said Aaron despondently. "What did you do?"

"What could I do?" said Grandpa Moshe. "Of course, for many months, I had nothing. I was a barely a man. I had only Miriam. But I realized quickly that I had no other purpose in life other than to care for our daughter, and to continue the work. Even more than before, I committed myself to the society of Lazarus."

"Is that what it's called?" asked Aaron. "The Society of Lazarus?"

"No," said Grandpa Moshe. "No, the society has no name. Only those who are members know of its existence."

"How does it work?" asked Aaron.

"The society has one goal," said Miriam, "to tell the truth."

Aaron guffawed, almost against his will, but he caught himself.

"What?"

"I'm sorry," said Aaron. "But that does seem a little ironic, doesn't it—given that you dress up like an old man and tell embellished stories?"

"Aaron, Aaron. You have steeped too long in the rationalist pot," said Grandpa Moshe. "You have forgotten what you knew when you were just a child—what we all know when we are children. All the greatest truths known to humankind are told through fables. Myths and miracles, legends and parables, Shakespeare and Dante, the fairy tales of our youth—all that we know deep down to be true, and all that we have known for millennia, sits behind a veil."

"Lazarus is a sort of ruse, yes," said Miriam, "but it is a ruse that is deadly serious. Truth is always under assault, as much today as ever before. Lazarus is a knight sent into the world to defend truth's honor. Lazarus tells the stories not only of the Jewish people, and of Jewish persecution, but the history of all people and all persecution. And that is the only goal. No nefarious plots are being hatched. There are no secret handshakes or smoke-filled rooms. We don't prop up candidates for congress. We don't even have a political party! Our lone goal is to preserve the historical record, to preserve truth."

"How does it work, then?" asked Aaron.

"Very simply, in a way," said Grandpa Moshe. "Only those with the utmost integrity are invited to meet Lazarus. The qualifications are vast, and nothing is more important than character. The numbers are extremely limited. They must be."

The Rise of Lazarus

"Is it only people from universities?"

"No, not at all. We look only for the ability to influence in a positive way. You need not have money or social status, even if those assets are common among those who have the power to influence other people. Tonight, for instance, all different types of people were in that room. There was a professor, and a headmaster from a prep school; one woman was a politician, and another was a doctor; a rabbi and a pastor; a vice admiral from the navy. Who else?"

"Let's see," said Miriam, "a woman from a hedge fund, a district attorney, a man from a town board in a rural area of Connecticut. They are all prominent people in their communities, people prominent because of their character."

"Only one or two people had not been there before," said Grandpa Moshe. "We never have more than one or two new members at a time. The network is not at all large."

"I don't mean to be offensive," said Aaron, "but I'm trying to understand. This is propaganda, essentially, right? You influence the influencers."

"You can call it that if you wish," said Grandpa Moshe. "I would challenge you to come up with any form of information that can't be deemed propaganda. But true propaganda must inspire action, must support a cause. We have no ax to grind. This is not a movement. We only hope to create some movement here."

Grandpa Moshe reached out and tapped Aaron on the chest.

"We are not supporting some faction, or some uprising," he went on. "Our business is not revolution. We are giving tools to humanity to combat its worst enemy, which is also here."

Grandpa Moshe again tapped Aaron on the chest.

"Our worst enemies are not each other," he said. "They are not out there in the world. Murder and genocide, persecution and torture: they are right here inside of us all."

Aaron was silent. He considered the words of his grandfather—the words of a man who had experienced the worst of humanity.

"And as I said earlier," added Miriam. "Lazarus, in a way, is not a lie. Lazarus, in a way, is still very much alive."

Chapter Twenty-Eight

The Seed of Lazarus

"I still don't understand," said Aaron. "What does it mean? How can Lazarus be alive?"

Miriam opened her mouth to speak, but Grandpa Moshe raised his hand to quiet her. He rocked himself forward out of his chair and went back to the mantlepiece to retrieve the photograph of the family. He sat down next to Aaron on the couch.

"Science has only begun to unravel the profound mysteries of our physical existence on this earth. As David says in the Psalm, God knit us together in the mother's womb. There are so many things we cannot see in a photograph. We cannot see the cancer that was growing in my dear Deborah's body. Nor can we see in a photograph that a woman's body contains generations.

"Look here," said Grandpa Moshe, pointing to the women. "There is your mother Miriam, the baby, and there is her mother, Deborah, and there is her mother, Marta. And all three of them at one time were contained in the flesh of Marta—in her daughter Deborah, and in her baby daughter's eggs, the future flesh of Miriam. Astounding, isn't it?"

"Mindboggling," said Aaron.

"The complexity of the genetic code—human past, present and future written into our lives—how can we understand it?"

Aaron tiredly blinked and shook his head in defeat, and Grandpa Moshe set down the photograph on the coffee table.

"Have you ever read the book of John?" he asked Aaron.

Aaron puzzled. The words echoed in his head. Professor Freeman had asked him the same question only a few weeks earlier, before his world had changed forever. The passage from John that Aaron had read was still fresh in his mind, the story of Lazarus. And yet he could not draw out the connection.

"I've read part of it," said Aaron. "I read the story of Lazarus. Professor Freeman asked me to read it."

"Very interesting," said Grandpa Moshe.

"Why?"

"Tell me this, Aaron. Do the names Marta and Miriam bring anything to mind?"

Aaron rolled his eyes, thinking, and slowly shook his head.

"Obviously, you know the equivalent of the name Marta."

"Martha?"

"Correct. And the name Miriam is the Hebrew version of what name?"

"I don't know," said Aaron.

"Mary."

Aaron put the names together in his head.

"Martha and Mary," said Aaron's mother. "Mary and Martha."

"The sisters of Lazarus," said Aaron.

Miriam and Grandpa Moshe nodded their heads.

"What does it mean?"

"We named your mother Miriam for two reasons," said Grandpa Moshe. "The first, you will recognize. We named her after the Miriam of ancient Egypt, the prophetess, the faithful sister who watched after her brother Moses as he floated among the reeds in the Nile."

"Moshe," said Miriam.

Aaron nodded.

"Moses was sent by God to Egypt to bring truth and justice, to deliver the Jews from slavery. When Pharaoh's command went out to murder all the firstborn sons of the Israelites, Miriam secured the life of Moses. She made sure he survived. Miriam is a protector, Aaron, and so is your mother. She is a protector of truth, a protector of history. She has given her whole life to this cause. That is the first reason. The second is much simpler, in a way."

Grandpa Moshe had a gleam in his eye.

"What is it?"

"Mary and Martha are family names."

"What?"

Miriam put her hand on Aaron's shoulder. He stared back at her in confusion.

"Aaron," she said, "you are born into this."

"Your great-grandmother Marta was not only dressing up as Lazarus," explained Grandpa Moshe. "She was, in a way, the same flesh and blood. Marta was a descendent of Martha, the sister of Lazarus. She was of the line of Lazarus. Your mother, Aaron, is a descendant of Lazarus. You, Aaron, are a descendant of Lazarus."

"You asked," said Miriam, "how far back this goes. Now you know, Aaron. Lazarus never died. Ever since the first century, the descendants of Mary and Martha have kept the fire burning. Over the centuries, this society has taken on many forms. Just as in the Order of Tabitha, we have no written rules. We have only a purpose."

Aaron was silent. He dropped his head. Grandpa Moshe elbowed him in his ribs, and a wide smile illuminated his face.

"We got our own family business!"

Aaron laughed, but he was awestruck. What they were saying was incredible. He was thrown into disarray not just by the information, but by the possible implications.

"You're overwhelmed," said Miriam. "That is as it should be. But don't be disheartened."

"What am I supposed to do?" said Aaron.

"You must not misunderstand. We are not giving you a task. We are not strapping a burden to your back. Remember, we did not intend to tell you any of this until much later."

"I know," said Aaron. "But I want to help. I want to learn. I want to study. I want to commit myself. I have wasted so much time."

"You can't learn all there is to know in one day," said Miriam. "More importantly, you cannot prepare your soul overnight. You were not born into a club for smart people, you were born into a calling. You were born to use your intellectual gifts for the good of humanity."

"Think of the parables," said Grandpa Moshe. "Just as the suitor in the parable, you must strive for knowledge and reason, for courage and selflessness, for faith and spirituality, for a disregard of worldly treasure and glory. These are not just cornerstones of religion; these are cornerstones of humanity."

Aaron nodded, taking their words to heart.

"But it is more complicated than that," continued Grandpa Moshe. "As the woodworker in the parable, you must strive for these things without striving. Only when you have trained yourself in that practice will you be prepared for the role you will play."

"What role is that?" asked Aaron.

"Only God knows."

Grandpa Moshe stood up from the couch and embraced Aaron. Miriam, too, embraced Aaron. Both had tears in their eyes.

"I will offer the morning prayer," said Grandpa Moshe. "For this is a new day."

Grandpa Moshe placed one hand on Aaron's shoulder and one hand on Miriam's shoulder. He bowed his head.

"We offer thanks to the living and eternal God, for you have restored our souls to us. Great is your faithfulness."

Chapter Twenty-Nine

A New Day

In the morning, Aaron came downstairs to find his mother and grandfather in their bathrobes at the dining room table. They were sitting quietly, sipping from their mugs of coffee. Aaron again had the sensation that he had been dreaming. In a few short weeks, his life had been turned upside down. But he also felt invigorated in a way he had never experienced. He was alert and eager, and his energy was not superficial. He was filled with a deep vitality, an ambition rooted in his being. New air was in his lungs.

Aaron selected a mug from the cabinet. Balancing his coffee out in front of him, he smiled and nodded at his mother and grandfather and walked out of the kitchen. In the living room, he set down his mug on the table and went to the bookshelf. Cocking his head to the side, he ran his fingers along the bindings, reading the titles. He settled on a book he had seen his mother reading recently, the journals of a Jewish scholar, born in Poland, who had lived in Germany throughout the period of the Third Reich.

Aaron opened the book on the table and quickly became absorbed. Every now and then, he sipped from his coffee mug, without taking his eyes off the page. After half an hour, Miriam peeked into the living room. She paused in the doorway, struck by his concentration. She remembered Aaron as he had been as a child, poring over his illustrated books on geology and medieval warfare. Grandpa Moshe soon was interested. He quietly came up behind Miriam and snuck a glance into the living room. After a moment, he shrugged at his daughter and shuffled away. Aaron did not notice either of them.

Another half an hour later, Miriam returned to the living room with a bowl of yogurt and granola. Without a word, she set the bowl down on the table. Only then did Aaron pick his head up from the book, awaking from a stupor.

"Oh. Thank you," he said.

Miriam disappeared again, and Aaron returned to his book, his curiosity insatiable. He read as if running out of time. In the late morning, Grandpa Moshe poked his head into the living room. Aaron was still reading contentedly.

"We should probably get going soon."

Aaron looked up, his jaw hanging slightly. He said nothing.

"To get you back to campus," said Grandpa Moshe.

"Oh, right. Yeah. I'm ready to go."

"I'm sure your mother wouldn't mind if you borrow the book. I believe the second volume is upstairs. Twenty minutes?"

Aaron nodded. He dropped his head over the open book as Grandpa Moshe retreated. By the time Grandpa Moshe returned half an hour later, Aaron had nearly finished the book. Holding his place with his thumb, he brought his bowl and mug back to the kitchen. His mother was at the dining room table, her computer open in front of her, a stack of exam papers next to her. She held out the second volume of the book for Aaron to take. She kissed Aaron on the forehead and hugged him. She held him at arm's length.

"Remember," she said, "this is the work of a lifetime, not a day. It is the work of the head, and the heart."

Aaron accepted his mother's words and put the second volume under his arm.

"Be good," she said. "If I find out you've been telling some shiksa about your mom's underground library, you're dead."

"I see you're back to normal," he chuckled.

She cuffed Aaron on the back of the head as he followed his grandfather to the front door. Grandpa Moshe was waiting in the car down below in the driveway. Aaron joined him.

"All set?"

"Yep," said Aaron. "Never been more ready."

"Do me a favor and read that out loud for me, would you?"

"Where I left off?"

"That's right."

Aaron opened the book on his lap. Finding his place at one of the breaks between journal entries, he read to his grandfather as they drove back to campus. From time to time, Aaron paused to ask his grandfather about a reference or historical point. Other times, Grandpa Moshe asked him to hold so that he could explain something related. They went back and forth for the duration of the drive, tutor and student. When they had pulled off the highway, Grandpa Moshe waited for Aaron to get to a stopping point in the text.

"This is how it is done," he said. "This is how it has been done for centuries. Your mother and I sit in the library in the basement and go back and forth. You are not on your own, Aaron. Knowledge does not reside with any one person alone."

As they approached campus, passing through the small college town, Aaron closed the book and looked through the window. He was seeing the campus environs with new eyes. He noticed the rare books store in town as if for the first time. They drove along the bending campus road, lined with oaks planted a century before. The massive old trees were filled with tiny green leaves. When they turned onto the lane leading to his dormitory, the imposing gray stone buildings of the original quad came into view, unshakeable in the weight of their years.

Grandpa Moshe pulled into a parking spot in front of Aaron's dormitory. Neither of them moved at first. They stared ahead. After a bit, Grandpa Moshe let out a long sigh.

"Well," he said, "I suppose I'll probably be back next weekend. I told Michael I would meet with him again."

"That's right," said Aaron. "What are you going to tell him?"

"I'll think of something. I can tell him many important things, without telling him the most important things. For all his faults, whatever they may be, Michael has a role to play. I believe he is, at heart, a good man."

Aaron got out of the car, the two volumes of the journals he had borrowed in his hands. He went around to the other side and hugged his grandfather.

"There's one thing I still don't quite get," said Aaron.

"What's that?"

"You said that no one meets Lazarus by mistake. How did Professor Freeman find out about all this? How was he invited to hear Lazarus speak?"

"I cannot say," said Grandpa Moshe, "but I will tell you again: no one meets Lazarus by mistake. I cannot understand how Michael Freeman was invited to meet Lazarus, and I cannot understand how he became your professor, and I cannot understand why you went to have coffee with him, but I know that all these things are orchestrated. All things happen for a reason."

Grandpa Moshe got back in the car. He rolled down the window and leaned over to open the glove compartment. He handed Aaron a folded piece of paper.

"Take this," he said. "This will get you started, if you're interested. No pressure."

"Thank you," said Aaron. "Thanks for everything."

Grandpa Moshe smiled and rolled up the window. Aaron stood in the parking lot with the folded paper. He watched his grandfather's car disappear.

Chapter Thirty

His Name is Barnabas

Aaron took his book to the dining hall that evening. He sat in a back corner with a plate of pasta, a fork in one hand, open book in the other. After dinner, he went to the library and set to work on his reading for class. For the first time since arriving at college, he was determined to complete all the reading for the week, in all his classes. He worked diligently through the evening, taking careful notes as he went along.

The next day, he woke early. After breakfast, he went to the library with the syllabi from all his classes. He looked up the books on the suggested reading list for his courses and brought them back to a table. Then he brought out the folded piece of paper his grandfather had given him. Grandpa Moshe had written out a list of books, some of them general history by professional historians, and some of them personal accounts such as journals and letters, from various historical periods, from various places around the world. Whatever books he could find, he brought back to his desk.

He sat down and surveyed the assortment. Learning had always seemed a chore to Aaron, despite the incredible ease with which he retained information. A stack of academic tomes had represented a pile of heavy stones that simply had to be moved from one place to another. Now the prospect of diving into the books in front of him was enticing, even exhilarating. He realized that, maybe for the first time, he had a purpose. He had a reason to gain knowledge. The task of reading, of learning, was in no way daunting. He wasn't aimlessly moving a pile of stones, he was stacking them, building them up, slowly constructing a fortress.

Aaron slid out one of the books and spun it around in front of him. As he did so, he felt a pat on his shoulder.

"I can see you're already hard at work," said Professor Freeman. "What brings you here so early on a Monday morning?"

"I'm finally doing my homework," said Aaron.

"It would seem so. That's no small stack."

"Too many books, too little time."

"I'd guess you're inspired," said the professor. "Maybe I know why."

"Maybe."

Professor Freeman walked around to the other side of the table. He pulled his bag off his shoulder and swung it onto the table. He sat down across from Aaron, tilting his head to read the bindings.

"Ah, I see you've even taken out a couple of the suggested books for my course. That should earn you some extra credit—not that you particularly need it at the moment. Is your grandfather still in town?"

"He's home. But he said he'll be back next weekend."

"Good. I'm looking forward to that," said Professor Freeman. "You see, there was one other part of your grandfather's story that I found especially intriguing, something I really wanted to ask him about."

Professor Freeman pulled his bag toward him and reached inside. He brought out an envelope with a button-and-string fastener.

"I have one other thing I wanted to show you both."

He began to unwind the string and stopped.

"Let me ask you, Aaron. Have you ever read the book of Acts?"

"I can't say that I have," said Aaron.

"It is a fascinating book—a book of history, really. I must recommend you read it some time. But there is one story in that book that I must tell you about. In fact, there is one character in that book that I must tell you about. His name is Barnabas."

About the Author

B. W. Jackson writes short stories and novels. His work has appeared in publications across the United States and in the United Kingdom. The next two books in the *Lazarus* series are forthcoming from Speaking Volumes. He lives outside New York City with his wife.

Upcoming New Release!

THE BROTHERHOOD OF BARNABAS
The Rise of Lazarus
Book Two

By
B. W. Jackson

Have you ever read the book of Acts? Just when Professor Freeman begins to uncover another eerie mystery, he suddenly goes missing, leaving Aaron and Grandpa Moshe and Miriam on a desperate mission to track him down. Along the way, they encounter the ancient origins of the Brotherhood of Barnabas and the rise of an enemy organization known as the Crimson Ribbon. Dubious clues lure them into a precarious adventure to the Old World, amidst the living history of Lazarus and Tabitha. But their quest is upended when a secret from the past is resurrected, challenging everything they thought they knew about the legend of Lazarus.

**For more information
visit:** www.SpeakingVolumes.us

Now Available!

GERI SPIELER

Regina of Warsaw
Book One

Winner of the 2024 New York Book Festival Award

"...inspired by historical events. A carefully crafted and simply riveting read from start to finish…" —*Midwest Book Review*

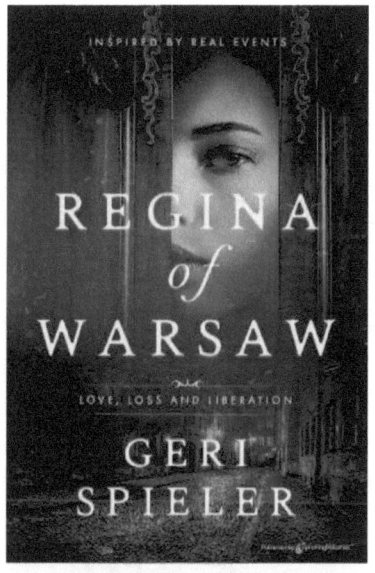

**For more information
visit: www.SpeakingVolumes.us**

Now Available!

ANNE SHAW HEINRICH

The Women of Paradise County
Book One

"...a captivating book that touches your heart and leaves a lasting impression. This beautifully crafted story will deeply resonate with you emotionally, as its characters will leave a lasting impression."

—*Midwest Book Review*

**For more information
visit:** www.SpeakingVolumes.us

www.ingramcontent.com/pod-product-compliance
Lightning Source LLC
LaVergne TN
LVHW041704060526
838201LV00043B/574